"So I'm finally through to y

Carlo's eyes gleamed in triumph. "No, *mia cara*, there is no conference." He smiled maliciously. "You are here at my express command, and strictly for my benefit. This villa is mine and you are—" he hesitated, choosing his words carefully "—my houseguest for the moment."

Helen stared at him numbly. Never in all her life had she felt so defenseless. "Why, Carlo? I know you hated my parents, but they're both dead now."

"You think there's no reason, do you?" His dark eyes blazed with anger. "To lose one *fidanzata* because of your father was insult enough, but two—I am Sicilian and remember an insult, *cara*. Now that he cannot steal you away from me, I will keep you here."

JACQUI BAIRD hails from Northeast England. She is married and has two sons. She especially enjoys traveling, and has many more ideas bubbling away in her head for books to follow *Dark Desiring*, her first Harlequin Presents novel.

JACQUI BAIRD

---

dark desiring

Harlequin Books

TORONTO • NEW YORK • LONDON
AMSTERDAM • PARIS • SYDNEY • HAMBURG
STOCKHOLM • ATHENS • TOKYO • MILAN

Harlequin Presents first edition June 1988
ISBN 0-373-11079-0

Original hardcover edition published in 1988
by Mills & Boon Limited

CHAPTER ONE

THE aircraft was like nothing Helen had ever seen before. She unfastened her seat-belt and stood up, gazing around her in amazement. Thick-piled carpet covered the floor, large cushioned chairs in black leather were grouped around low tables, and in one corner there was a well stocked bar. The whole cabin was the last word in comfort. She turned to her companion, her green eyes sparkling with excitement.

'I thought we would be going on a scheduled flight. I've never seen anything like this outside the movies! Who on earth does it belong to?'

The young man stood at the bar, and studied the girl who was looking around in such awe. She really was very lovely. Tall, about five foot eight, with long blonde hair piled on top of her head in a chignon, revealing the clear lines of her face and throat. The cream trousers she wore clung enticingly to her fantastically long legs, the matching camisole top barely concealed the tender curve of her full breasts, and a blouson jacket draped casually over her shoulders completed the picture. For the first time since he had met her, he actually questioned if he was doing the right thing. She looked so innocent, damn it ... He raised his glass to his mouth and drained it. Well, it soon wouldn't be his problem.

A grim smile twisted his lips as he answered, 'It belongs to my uncle; he was a keen pilot at one time. But now it's mostly used for ferrying tired executives around.'

'Well, it's gorgeous,' Helen opined, sinking down into one of the soft chairs.

The last time she had visited sicily, she had been with her father; a small sigh escaped her at the memory. He had been a Professor of Ancient Roman History, and

5

leader of a working party, excavating part of a Roman villa near the medieval town of Piazza Armerina. Her mother had died when she was born and, consequently, Helen had been much closer to her father than most young girls. From the age of eight, she had spent every school holiday travelling with him, either in Italy or Sicily. The last time had been when she was fourteen. The following year he had refused to take her with him, and had gone on his own, returning in September with Maria, his new wife. The next spring, her stepbrother, Andrea, was born. They had never gone back to Sicily again, and it wasn't till she was eighteen that she had found out why. Pushing the unpleasant memories away, she glanced at her boss, Stephano Alviani, and had to smile. In repose, he didn't look much older than her brother, Andrea.

She remembered her surprise the first time she had met the young Italian at her job interview. He had not looked anything like she imagined an advertising executive should look like, but more like a pop star. And when he'd spoken...

'You are even lovelier than he said.'

Helen, completely confused, had murmured back, 'Then who said?'

'I'm sorry, Miss Coulthard, you must forgive me. It was Miss Thomas. She described you to me. Unfortunately, I tend to get my genders mixed in English. Though only when speaking,' he added, grinning wickedly.

Helen had laughed nervously, thinking there was no doubt about the truth of his statement; anyone more blatantly male would be hard to find. It was Miss Thomas, the head of the secretarial college, who had arranged the interview, saying she had been asked to provide a bilingual secretary, and Helen had been the obvious choice, being fluent in both Italian grammar and vocabulary, and having only one week of her course to complete.

She loved her job. and the last two months at Garston's Advertising had done a lot to help her finally get over her grief at losing her father and stepmother in a car accident the previous August. A year ago last weekend had been the first anniversary of their death. Mary, the girl whose office she shared, and Pete, Mary's fiancé had been very supportive, and they had all become firm friends.

Pete was always warning her, what a wolf and a romeo her boss was. Every model who walked into the agency, Stephano made a date with. Pete was convinced that the takeover of the company, a couple of weeks before Helen had started working there, had been arranged simply to give Stephano easy access to all the models. It had become a standing joke in the office. In fact no one knew exactly who had bought the firm.

Personally, Helen thought Stephano a bit of a pussycat. They quite often went out together to business luncheons and dinners, and he was always the perfect gentleman. Helen was supposed to be his interpreter, but she felt a bit of a fraud, as Stephano spoke very good English.

Leaning her head back against the seat, Helen yawned widely. The last two days had been pretty hectic.

On Thursday evening, she had attended a reception at the Italian Embassy with her boss. They had met another couple there: Diego Fratelli, a business friend of Stephano's, whom Helen had met before and found charming, and his not-so-charming girlfriend, Caterina Belgosa, a gorgeous brunette, several years older than Helen. It had turned out to be a long night. They went on to the Savoy for dinner, and finally ended up at Stringfellow's. Helen had found the evening a strain as the older woman appeared to take an instant dislike to her and made no attempt to disguise the fact. To top it all, Helen remembered over dinner where she had seen Caterina before. Just that morning, on the gossip page of one of the more infamous national newspapers, there had been a photo of Caterina leaving Rome airport, but the object of the picture was the man seeing her off. Carlo Manzitti, the elusive Italian industrialist, and someone Helen had spent the last two years determinedly trying to forget existed. So it had been a relief when the evening had ended, though, thinking about it now, she realised Stephano had behaved rather oddly.

Diego had suggested they all meet again on the Saturday night, and Helen had been delighted that she had a genuine excuse for refusing. She had promised to go on a sailing weekend with her friend Robbie. Stephano was not at all pleased, and with a brief goodnight to the other pair, had hustled her out of the club, and home to the old stone farmhouse, she shared with her Gran and Andrea in Kent.

The following morning, on arriving at the office, Helen had been amazed to find Stephano already there. It was unheard of; he never started work before eleven normally. Then he had dropped his bombshell.

He had to attend a conference in Palermo for two weeks, and she was to go with him. He had arranged for them to leave on the Saturday morning, and told her to have the rest of the day off to pack. He would call for her at eight-thirty and reassure her Gran that she would be well looked after, and that was it. Before Helen could take in what he was telling her, he had turned on his heel and left, only reminding her, as he went out of the door, not to forget her passport.

Helen looked out of the window, the sun glinting on the plane's wings dazzling her eyes. Then Sicily appeared, dreamlike, beneath them. She was surprised at how quickly the flight had passed. Mount Etna stood, stark and dominating at the eastern end of the island. The black lava-flows and small craters were clearly visible near the top, tapering into the vineyards and lush citrus groves lower down the slopes, making a brilliant contrast with their vibrant colours.

They landed at Palermo airport. Taking Helen's passport, Stephano whisked them through Customs, and in a matter of minutes they were outside the airport, and he was introducing her to an elderly man standing next to a gleaming white Mercedes. Helen acknowledged the introduction with a wide smile. Then, taking a deep breath, she inhaled the hot, scented air. She remembered the scent of the island so well: a mixture of wine and flowers with the tang of the peculiar toasted tobacco, so popular with the Sicilians. Seated in the back seat of the car, she could not take her eyes off the passing scenery. Flowers grew everywhere, the red, pink and white of oleanders and geraniums surrounded stucco-washed cottages that sparkled almost orange in the brilliant sunlight, while others were masked completely by vividly coloured creepers.

They were travelling down a steep, tree-lined road, when it occurred to her that she did not know where they were staying. Swinging round in her seat, she asked Stephano, 'You haven't told me where we're staying in Palermo.' Then added, 'Surely we should be there by now?'

'Oh, didn't I tell you? We aren't staying in Palermo, but... at a friend's villa. You'll love it. There's a swimming...'

Helen never heard the rest of his statement, as she caught her breath in wonder at the view before them. The car had swung around and stopped in front of a long white building, set into the hillside and facing straight out over a small cove. It was the loveliest house she had ever seen.

Climbing out of the car, she stared in open-mouthed awe. The villa was designed in three tiers, and graceful Moorish arches ran along the front, supporting the terrace and floors above. The overall effect was breathtaking, like ribbons of white lace sparkling in the sunlight. A plaque in the centre of the first floor bore the year, but as yet no name. Obviously, the place was brand-new. The gardens were terraced, going down in glorious bands of coloured vegetation to stop at a large stone sea wall, with an intricately worked, wrought-iron gate, opening on to a small sandy beach and the sea.

The place seemed vaguely familiar, but, before she could pursue the thought, Stephano took her arm and led her into the house. The hall was large, with a curving marble staircase at the end. The floor, a highly polished mosaic in cream and green with darker insets, formed an eyecatching design. She had a fleeting glimpse, through a partly opened door, of an elegant panelled dining-room, then Stephano was introducing her to a small plump lady, dressed in the almost mandatory black.

'This is Sophia, Tommaso's wife and the housekeeper.'

Helen smilingly acknowledged the older woman, and was rewarded by a beaming grin, revealing the most startling set of false teeth Helen had ever seen. Stephano continued rather apologetically, explaining that he had to leave immediately, but Sophia had prepared lunch for her and, if there was anything else she wanted, she only had to ask. Without giving Helen a chance to query his statement, he turned on his heel and left.

There was nothing for it but to meekly follow Sophia up the large marble staircase, and into what was to be her room for the length of her stay. Helen was more than a little confused by the speed with which everything had happened, and was glad to sit down on the bed for a moment, trying to assimilate all she had seen.

The room was beautiful, decorated all in white and gold. The bed, a large four-poster, was draped in the finest white lace, with a matching cover. High arched windows led out on to the terrace, running the length of the house.

A rumbling in her stomach reminded Helen she had not eaten for some time. Standing up, she crossed the room to the only other door and, opening it, found herself in the en-suite bathroom. Again, it was all in white and gold. Shrugging out of her clothes, she had a quick shower, then, wrapping a large fluffy towel, sarong-style, around her body, she returned to the bedroom.

Opening her suitcase, she found a brief white bikini and pulled it on, quickly slipping the matching cotton shift-dress over the top. She loosened her hair from its restraining chignon and, flicking it behind her ears, swiftly made her way downstairs.

Sophia was waiting in the hall, and led Helen through a side door, out on to the patio. A table was set under a large umbrella, with a selection of cold meats and a crisp salad. Half a carafe of wine stood next to a single place setting. Thanking Sophia, Helen sat down and set to with gusto.

By the time she had finished eating and drunk a couple of glasses of wine, she felt completely relaxed, and rather sleepy. The pool was a few steps down from the patio, circular and inviting, with garden furniture scattered around it.

Walking down to the poolside, she removed her dress, dropping it on the nearest table. Then, with a sigh of pure bliss, she stretched out on the conveniently placed lounger.

Helen flicked her leg with a slender hand, only half awake; the irritation was probably some insect strolling over her thigh. Her eyes fluttered, reluctant to open; there it was again. She opened her eyes wider, stretching her young body sensuously in the warmth of the afternoon sun, her hand again rubbing her thigh.

She sat up with a jerk. That was no insect, but someone else's hand! Instantly she was wide awake. It had to be Stephano, fooling around.

'Stephano, behave...' She stopped, thunderstruck, gazing in amazement at the man standing over her.

He was huge, or so it seemed from her position on the lounger, standing with his back to the sun. She could not see his features clearly, but his size alone told her it wasn't her boss. Then he moved slightly to one side, and Helen's eyes widened even further.

Thick black hair tinged with silver was swept carelessly to one side, across a broad forehead. Rather long, it curled around his ears to brush the collar of his shirt at the back. The top few buttons of his silk shirt were open, revealing a broad, tanned, hair-roughened chest, tapering to a narrow waist. Black trousers curved and clung tightly to his lean hips, his muscular thighs clearly defined beneath the taut material, as he stood, hands in pockets, like a modern-day reincarnation of some pagan god.

He was not conventionally handsome, but the force of his personality was evident in every line of his face. Black brows arched over heavy-lidded dark eyes. His nose was straight but rather large; deep grooves cut into the tanned skin from nose to mouth; his lips were firm, the bottom one slightly fuller—evidence of his sensuous nature.

A quiver of fear shot through Helen's body, as she recognized him and for the first time noticed the jagged scar at his temple. Carlo Manzitti! Her hand flew to her mouth, and silently she screamed, no... No, it can't be!

His voice, low and harsh, broke the tense silence. 'So, Helena, we meet again. It's been a long time.'

At the sound of his voice, her worst nightmares were realised. How could she ever have hoped to forget him? she thought, swinging her legs off the lounger. Her one idea was to get away, but she was too late. Strong brown hands snaked out and caught her arms, hauling her to her feet. His dark head swooped, his mouth covering hers in a brutal kiss. Kaleidoscopic pictures of another time flashed through her mind, and memories she had painfully blanked out for so long came rushing back to haunt her.

His hands sensually caressed her almost naked body, roaming at will from her shoulders to her thighs. Helen, frozen in shock, offered no resistance as his mouth ravaged hers and forced her lips to part to the invasion of his tongue. One strong hand curved around her hip, sliding across the flat plane of her stomach, his fingers probing beneath the thin material of her bikini.

Helen trembled uncontrollably in his arms, and fear shot through her at his intimate touch, bringing her back to reality. She jerked away from him, flinging her head back at the same time, to avoid his mouth.

'No...No! Please,' she cried.

Her voice seemed to get through to him, and his dark eyes narrowed, as he studied her terror-filled face.

Then, in a low voice and harsh with anger, he grated, 'I've waited two years for this, and you aren't going to stop me now.'

Helen was terrified, emotions long suppressed stirred in her body, and her heart beat frantically against his chest as he held her firmly against him.

'You didn't really think I would let you get away from me so easily, did you, Helena? You should know that what's mine I keep. And you are mine, aren't you, *cara*?' he drawled.

His sarcastic endearment rasped on her already quivering nerves, and fear lay like lead in her stomach. She could not answer, for her mind was in turmoil, her body traitorously aware of every muscular inch of the man who held her.

'What, nothing to say?' he derided, his dark gaze never leaving her face.

Nervously, she ran the tip of her tongue over dry lips. 'Please, Carlo...Please, let me go!' Her eyes were huge and pleading in the deathly pallor of her face.

His voice took on a mocking tone, showing that he was fully aware of how he had affected her. 'Is that all you can say, Helena, after all this time?' Not waiting for an answer, he continued, 'Why should I let you go? I enjoy the feel of your delectable body against mine and, as I remember it, you were never averse to my caresses in the past. Quite the opposite, in fact.'

Letting go of her wrists, his hand slid down to her buttocks, pulling her hard into the curve of his hips. 'What's the matter, Helena? Does my scarred face frighten you?'

'No... No, of course not,' she whispered, opening her eyes. 'How did it happen?' she asked, more to give herself a breathing space than from any real desire to know, but she wished she hadn't when he answered her.

'My, such concern!' he mocked. 'But rather late. I could have used that the night you ran out on me. I drove back to Rome with slightly less than one hundred per cent concentration, and crashed the car. Hardly surprising under the circumstances, I'm sure you'll agree.'

Helen stood motionless, unable to say a word. The protective shell she had painstakingly developed over the past two years was cracked wide open by the reappearance of this man, and by what he had told her. He had dominated her almost completely once before. She had been unable to refuse him then, hadn't wanted to, and she wasn't at all sure of her ability to resist him now.

Two years ago, on holiday near Rome with her family, she had met Carlo Manzitti, and fallen madly in love with him, and he with her, or so he had led her to believe. Love's young dream had lasted eight short days, before she had learnt the truth, and been bitterly disillusioned. She could not think why he was here now. No sooner had the thought entered her head than she was blurting it out.

'I can't understand how you're here, or why. I never wanted you...'

He did not let her finish the sentence. His handsome face twisted with rage. 'So, you never wanted me? Perhaps I should remind you just what it is you don't want,' he drawled silkily, his dark gaze unwavering on her pale face. For the life of her Helen couldn't break the contact. Gently, his long fingers brushed the tangled mass of golden hair from her brow. Then his mouth was on hers, but softly now. Sweetly, sensuously, he kissed and caressed her, one hand lightly stroking over the soft swell of her breast as he eased her down on to the lounger.

To Helen, this deliberate seduction of her senses was a hundred times more dangerous than his anger. He was arousing long forgotten, deeply buried feelings and desires she did not want to recognize. Vainly she tried to squirm from him. She lifted her hands, clasping his arms in a feeble attempt at restraining him, but the feel of his warm flesh only heightened her awareness of him. His long fingers found the ribbon of her bikini top, and tugged it loose. His breathing was harsh to her ears, and her own breath checked in her throat, as he raised himself on one elbow, and looked down on her nakedness.

'God, you're so beautiful, Helena,' he murmured, lowering his head slowly as he spoke. One brown hand gently cupped the creamy fullness of her breast, his thumb teasing the pink tip to instant tautness, while his tongue licked lightly over its partner with the same shattering effect.

Helen groaned, more in desire than terror. She closed her eyes, the musky male scent of him filling her nostrils, his breath hot on the soft swell of her breast. This could not be happening, it was a nightmare! But, when his mouth closed over the hard tip teasing the nipple with tongue and teeth, she was lost. The flame of desire raced through her veins, her own heartbeat sounding like a drum in her head, then merciful blackness enveloped her.

Helen opened her eyes to find Carlo standing over her, a glass in his hand.

'Here, drink this. It will make you feel better. Too much sun...or something...' he mocked, handing her the glass of amber liquid.

She sat up slowly and took the drink he offered, gulping it down quickly, only to cough violently, almost choking, as she realised it was brandy.

She must have fainted, and wondered vaguely how long she had been unconscious. She flushed to the roots of her hair as she remembered what had preceded her faint, and hastily looked down. Her bikini top was back in place. She supposed she should be grateful, but she certainly wasn't about to thank him, she thought grimly, putting the glass down on the ground.

Warily, she watched him as he pulled up the chair opposite, and sank down on it, his long legs stretched smoothly in front of him, his hands behind his head, completely relaxed. His dark face was expressionless, like some polite stranger. She could almost believe she had imagined the last half-hour.

She had to admit that he was still a very sexy man. The scar from his temple, curving slightly down one cheekbone, only added to his air of proud arrogance. He projected a raw virility that women the world over found irresistible. No wonder he was angry because she had run out on him. It wasn't because he cared about her, she told herself. It was simply a dent to his male ego.

She shivered, suddenly cold, and looked away towards the sea. Nothing had changed. The sun shone brilliantly in the clear blue sky, the water in the pool shimmered silver in its reflected rays, and the heady scent of the garden floated in the still air. No, nothing had changed in the last few minutes, except that her world had fallen apart.

CHAPTER TWO

CARLO'S cynically voiced, 'Well, Helena, I think perhaps you and I should have a little talk,' interrupted her thoughts.

'Yes, that would be wise,' she responded, unable to hide the bitterness she felt from her voice. There were quite a lot of questions she wanted to ask him: how he happened to be here, for starters. It was too incredible to be a coincidence. 'You must be a friend of Stephano's,' she stated, rather than questioned.

He faced her, brown eyes gleaming with mockery.

'Friend, uncle, boss, take your pick,' he offered.

'Stephano's your nephew?' Her eyes swept over him in surprise. Gradually, through the hazy confusion of the last half-hour, her mind was beginning to function again, and she did not like what it was telling her.

'The villa, who does it belong to?'

'Mine.'

Just one word, and it was enough to send fresh tremors of fear down her spine. She had to go on, still hoping she was wrong and it was all a terrible coincidence.

'Then you came here to meet Stephano. You didn't know I was here as his secretary?'

Carlo stretched lazily in his chair, and gazed out across the pool for ages, or so it seemed to the waiting girl. She guessed he was deliberately making her wait for his answer.

Coolly he turned towards her, his expression enigmatic.

'Much as I hate to disappoint a lady, I'm afraid I *did* know you were here. In fact, I arranged the whole trip. I bought Garston's expressly to give Stephano a valid cover to employ you, and bring you here to my home.

I must congratulate him, he has succeeded admirably. Though I don't think you were very hard to fool.'

Helen cringed at the sarcasm evident in his words. But he was right. The ease with which she had got the job, before her college course had finished, had been too good to be true. At the interview, Stephano had said, 'He told me you were lovely,' then masked his mistake by blaming his unsureness with the language; yet his English was almost perfect. The first week at work, when she found out that the firm had only been taken over a couple of weeks before, and nobody knew who by, was suspicious, but she hadn't thought so at the time. She glanced across at Carlo. Would he really have gone to that much trouble? Hesitantly she asked, 'Then the conference in Palermo is a fable?'

'So I am finally getting through to you!' A triumphant gleam sparked in the depths of his dark eyes. 'No, there is no conference, *cara*,' he drawled maliciously. 'You are here at my express command, and strictly for my benefit, so don't waste your time trying to kid yourself otherwise. This villa is mine and you are my...' He hesitated, choosing his words with exaggerated care. 'How shall I put it? My house guest, for the moment.'

Never in all her life had she felt so defenceless. This man hated her family, she knew; and, deep inside, she knew that perhaps he had some justification. His dark gaze never wavered from her flushed face, he was like some jungle cat with its prey and she was it...

The silence stretched between them, tension building unbearably in her shattered mind, till she was forced to speak.

'Why, Carlo? Why arrange to get me here? We haven't seen each other in almost two years.' She hesitated, waiting for some response, but one look at his icy expression had her stammering on. 'I-I know we parted a-angrily.' A vivid picture of their last meeting leapt to her mind. 'I know you wanted to get at father and Maria through me, but they're both dead now, so there's no reason for you to hate them any more.' Before she got out the last word, she knew she had made a mistake.

'So, there is no reason, you say!' His dark eyes blazed with anger. 'The fact you ran out on me, after the promise you made, the oh-so-sweet avowals of love, isn't that a good enough reason?' he mocked.

Helen twisted her slender fingers together in her lap, appalled by the bitterness she could sense in his words.

'To lose one *fidanzata* to your father was insult enough, but two... I am Sicilian, you should have remembered that. It was lucky for you that your father got you out of the country so quickly.' His lips curled back over his teeth in a mockery of a smile. 'And your luck is still holding, because I have decided to keep you instead.'

She closed her eyes for a second, the dull throbbing in her head getting worse by the minute, and she was shocked to her soul by his words. Gathering every bit of will-power she possessed, she opened her eyes and forced herself to face him. 'Keep me, Carlo! What do you mean?' she finally managed to ask, in a surprisingly steady voice.

'What do I mean? I think you know very well, *cara*. You will give me what Maria gave your father.'

'I don't understand you.'

'My dear Helena,' he drawled insolently. 'You are not quite so naïve as all that. You have a little brother.'

'Well, yes, but what has that got to do with anything?' she asked, puzzled, wondering how her stepbrother could possibly be of interest to Carlo Manzitti.

His dark brows rose in derision. 'So you wish to pretend the naïve innocent. Very well, I will explain.' Though it was obvious by his tone he believed she was being deliberately obtuse. 'My father is an old and rather sick man. He desires to see me married and have sons to carry on our name. A very natural wish, I'm sure you agree. If Maria had stayed here, instead of running off with your father, she would have had my child.' He added, cynically, 'Probably still be alive today. However, you're here, and eminently suitable.'

'How dare you say that?' Helen's green eyes flashed, 'Dad and Maria loved each other, something you know nothing about! The accident was tragic——' Her voice broke on the last word. Swallowing hard, she managed to control her emotions, but knowing there was some grain of truth in his last statement didn't help. Determinedly, she carried on. 'I don't know what your game is, Carlo, and I don't want to know. I'm leaving here just as soon as I can.' Anger gave her the strength to oppose him, letting him know that she was no longer the eighteen-year-old girl he had been able to control with a simply disapproving look.

Carlo slowly unfurled from the seat, and turned smartly away, calling over his shoulder as he made his way back to the house.

'I have some work to attend to. We will continue this conversation later. I suggest you go to your room and rest. As for leaving here, forget it. You aren't going anywhere.'

Only as he reached the house did Helen notice Sophia standing at the patio door. So that was the reason for her unexpected freedom.

Helen picked up her dress and slid into it. For a moment she had a wild urge to turn and run, anywhere to get away from him would do, she told herself, then just as quickly dismissed the idea, forcing herself to think rationally. To start with, she wasn't too sure where the villa was. They had not driven through Palermo on leaving the airport, but along country roads. Vaguely recalling the geography of the island, she guessed this cove must be somewhere near the gulf of Castellammare, but anyway it didn't make much difference, she was in no state to start what would be a very long walk to the nearest town. The heat was beginning to get to her and, unless she got to her room pretty quickly, her shaking legs would collapse beneath her.

Carlo was standing in the hall, talking on the telephone, his long body propped against the wall in negligent ease. Helen shot him a wary glance through lowered lashes, dashing past him to get to the stairs.

'Wait, Helena.'

She stopped, her foot on the first step, unsure whether to ignore him.

'We are dining tonight with my father, be ready at eight-thirty,' he demanded, then went back to his conversation, taking her acceptance for granted.

She continued upstairs without answering, inwardly fuming at the arrogance of the man. It was with a feeling of intense relief that she closed the bedroom door. The events of the day, especially the last hour, had left her completely exhausted. She sank down on the bed, and gazed with indifference around the beautiful room that had so entranced her only hours before.

Being honest, Helen had to admit that the man downstairs did have some justification for his angry behaviour towards her. Two years ago she had promised to marry him. They had even chosen the ring. Then, a couple of days later, she had run away from him. She had never expected to see him again, and right now she couldn't think of a thing to do about it. Recalling what he had told her about his car accident, the night she had left him, did not make her feel much better. The thought of Carlo lying injured, alone, and knowing she was indirectly responsible, horrified her.

She flopped down on the bed, flinging one arm across her eyes in a gesture of helplessness as the memories she had fought so hard to forget returned insidiously to haunt her.

It was the summer she had left school. The whole family was holidaying in a villa some half-hour's drive from Rome. Her father was away lecturing or visiting various digs during the week, only returning to the villa for the weekends. Maria, Andrea and herself had spent most of the time lazing around the swimming pool in general idleness.

It was near the end of their holiday when Gran had rung from England with Helen's exam results, telling her she had passed to go to university. Maria had decided they would go shopping in Rome the next day, Thursday, to celebrate.

They started at Valentino's, where Maria had bought Helen a totally impractical, terribly expensive emerald-green, silk trouser-suit. Then they had walked around for over an hour, finally ending up on the Via Condotti, perhaps the best known shopping street in the world. Eventually, footsore and weary, they were on the point of entering the Café Creco for coffee, when Helen heard, above the hurly burly of the street noises, a voice calling Maria. She caught her stepmother's arm and, turning swiftly, found herself slap up against an extremely tall man, with the deepest brown eyes she had ever seen.

He was looking straight down at Helen, one tanned hand holding her bare arm, while his perfectly defined lips curved in a warm smile as if he knew her.

She remembered it all as if it was yesterday. His magnificent physique was clad in an immaculate grey silk suit, and a brilliant white shirt with a darker tie, which contrasted starkly with his tanned face. Everything about him spelt wealth, down to his custom-made leather shoes. She should have realised then that there was something not quite right, as Maria introduced him.

'Helen, this is Carlo Manzitti.' She hesitated slightly. 'My brother's partner in the boatyard.' Turning to him as she spoke, 'Helen, my stepdaughter.'

'Hello, Signor Manzitti,' Helen managed to get out, overwhelmingly conscious of his warm hand on her arm.

He watched her, amused by her obvious embarrassment, and perfectly aware of the effect his potently masculine charms had on the female of the species.

'Oh, please call me Carlo. There's no need for your English formality.' He smiled. 'And I shall call you Helena. I am sure we are going to be friends, very good friends,' he opined in English, with barely a trace of an accent.

Helen never noticed how they came to be sitting at a table in a café, her arm still tingling from his touch, and it was the sound of Carlo's voice talking in rapid Italian that finally impinged on her consciousness.

In that moment, it was as though they were the only two people in the world. The noise and bustle around them disappeared. Something intangible was recognized and agreed between them. He reached out a strong hand and covered hers where it lay on the table, his dark head bent towards her...

'Good, our coffee.' Maria's voice broke the invisible thread of awareness between them.

Helen drew her hand away as if it was burnt. She must be going crazy, imagining things. Why would a gorgeous man like Carlo bother with her? He could have his pick of women, that was obvious just by looking around the room. All the females in the place seemed to be watching him.

'Is that all right with you, dear? I know how much you want to go sightseeing.' Not waiting for Helen's answer, Maria rattled on. 'But I'm not really interested, I've seen it all before, and anyway I have to be back at the villa by two, for Andrea. Carlo will make you a much better guide, and he will bring you home in time for dinner.'

That was how it had started...

Helen moved restlessly on the bed, her body hot at the memories flowing through her mind. She had been an absolute pushover for the sophisticated Carlo, but at the time she had naïvely believed he shared her feelings. It was not until later, much later, that she found out the truth.

God, how stupid she had been! Looking back, she wondered why Maria had not warned her. She, more than anyone, must have known how ruthless he was.

Over dinner that night, Maria had made little mention of Carlo, only pointing out that at thirty-four he was a lot older than Helen, so it would be wise not to mention going out with him to her father. It would only cause him to worry. After all, there was only one week of their holiday left, so nothing was likely to come of the friendship.

Helen had agreed, too much in a dream world of her own to wonder at Maria's statement. Carlo had told her he had to go to his father's birthday celebrations for the weekend, but he would be back on Monday, he had promised.

True to his word, he had turned up at the villa on Monday lunch time, and the next few days flew by in a rosy haze of pleasure for Helen. They toured Rome with a thoroughness that would have exhausted the most hardened courier, talking, laughing, occasionally stopping at a pavement café, and just watching the world go by.

The physical attraction between them had been intense. She only had to see him to want him. When he'd taken her home at night, the passionate kisses they'd exchanged had driven her crazy. He only had to touch her and she went up in flames. He had awakened her to a sensual side of her nature she hadn't known she possessed, and it was purely Carlo's iron self-control that stopped things getting out of hand...

On the Wednesday, Helen paid particular attention to her make-up as she prepared for the evening ahead. Carlo had arranged to take both her and Maria to an exclusive supper club on the outskirts of Rome, where Maria's brother Roberto would be joining them. As neither brother nor sister had met since Maria's marriage, it was in way of being a celebration.

With a sense of rising excitement, Helen slipped into the emerald silk trouser-suit Maria had bought her. The camisole top was too brief to allow the wearing of a bra, and clung lovingly to her high, full breasts. The trousers slid over her hips, accentuating her long legs beautifully. Surveying the finished effect in the chevalier mirror, she smiled. Her long hair, caught at each side of her head with silver combs, cascaded like a golden waterfall, past her shoulders. Surely tonight Carlo would see her as a sophisticated woman, she thought, as she turned and left the bedroom.

Carlo's reaction was everything she could have hoped for. As soon as she entered the lounge, he was at her side.

'You look beautiful, *cara*, but I'm not sure I like the idea of other men seeing you in that outfit. It's almost immoral.' His brown eyes gleamed possessively as he added, 'I think I'd better chain you to my side for the night.'

Roberto was waiting for them when they arrived, and the evening took on a party atmosphere. He turned out to be a great raconteur, and soon had them all laughing at his tall tales.

The two men chose the food for them all, and Carlo insisted on ordering champagne, saying it was a grand reunion, so nothing else would do.

Helen guessed Maria must have missed her brother a lot over the last few years, and wondered why they did not keep in closer touch. From odd hints that were dropped, she gathered Maria was not mad about Roberto's wife, so perhaps that was the reason. But all thoughts of the other couple fled out of her mind when Carlo's fingers laced with hers, and he gently pulled her on to the dance-floor.

She glided into his arms, like a bird coming home to roost. His strong arms folded around her, holding her closely against his hard frame, while her slender hands clasped around his neck, her fingers curling in his crisp black hair, every thought in her head X-rated.

They moved together in perfect unison to the slow, romantic music, and when Carlo led her out on to the terrace, his arm firmly around her waist, she made no objection.

The lights of Rome were spread before them, shining like a million multi-coloured stars, merging with the genuine article in the velvet sky. Helen caught her breath at the panorama before her, then Carlo was turning her round to face him. She looked up into his ruggedly attractive face, saying 'I have never seen anything more beautiful.'

'Wherever you are is beautiful to me, *cara*,' he voiced huskily. 'You must know how I feel about you. I swore to myself I would give you time to get to know me better before I said anything to you, but I can't wait any longer. I want you too much.' His hands slid from her waist to her hips, curving her pliant body into his hard, muscled thighs, making her achingly aware of his arousal. Then his lips claimed hers in a wildly passionate kiss.

'You will marry me,' Carlo rasped, demanding rather than asking, as his lips trailed a path of fire from her mouth to her slender throat.

Of course, she agreed. She was fathoms deep in love, and innocently told him so.

Remembering, Helen cringed with shame. Had she really been so easily duped. God! He must have laughed himself silly at how easily she had fallen, like a ripe plum, into his arms. How stupid she had been at eighteen to think that sexual arousal in a man was synonymous with love. She wasn't a lot more experienced now, but at least she had learned that much. Carlo was a very virile man; he probably turned it on with any attractive female. Damn him!

Maria and Roberto had interrupted them on the terrace. Roberto had been delighted at the news of their engagement, but Maria had been peculiarly silent. However, Helen had been too happy at the time to notice.

The following morning, Carlo had taken her to Bulgari's, the best jewellers in Italy, and they had chosen a magnificent emerald and diamond ring. It had been too large for her, so they had left it at the shop to be altered. Over an early lunch, they had discussed their plans. Carlo, unfortunately, had to return to Sicily that afternoon, to deal with some problems at the Marina, but he would be back on the Friday evening to talk to her father, and on the Sunday he would take her to Sicily to meet his family.

CHAPTER THREE

IT HAD been an uneven match from the start. Carlo was a dynamic man, possessing a degree of sexual expertise few women could resist, and certainly not the young Helen, as Carlo proved conclusively that last fatal Friday.

The sun beat down through a clear azure sky. It was a blisteringly hot day, and the rich scent of the garden flowers hung heavily on the still air. Helen, clad in a green wisp of a bikini, was lying on an airbed by the pool, half asleep.

She sat up, startled, when Carlo arrived. He wasn't supposed to be coming till the evening.

'No, don't get up. I will join you,' were the first words he spoke. Helen sank back on the airbed, smiling up at him.

'You're early.'

'So, are you complaining?' he derided, towering over her. He was wearing an open-necked, short-sleeved blue shirt and a pair of faded blue jeans that hugged his hips and thighs like a second skin. It was the first time she had seen him in anything other than a formal suit, and the air of shattering masculinity he wore like a cloak, that had so enveloped her at their first meeting, was even more pronounced by his casual attire, and threatened to overwhelm her completely.

'No, no,' she finally got out as, fascinated, she watched him unbutton his shirt and remove it, carelessly dropping it on the ground. Then his hands went to the stud of his jeans, and hesitated.

'We are alone here, I take it?' Carlo questioned, amusement evident in his tone. 'I've had enough of car parks, public monuments and terraces to last me a lifetime.'

Helen looked up at him, grinning. 'I know exactly what you mean. It's all right, no one will be back until this evening.' She had hardly finished speaking, before his jeans had joined his shirt on the ground.

Helen's green eyes widened in wonder. He was magnificent! His skin shone like dark gold satin in the afternoon sun. Slowly her gaze travelled over his wide shoulders and broad, hair-roughened chest, following the line of soft black body hair to his brief navy trunks, that fitted almost too snugly over narrow hips, accentuating the essential maleness of him. Hastily she brought her gaze back to his, a flush of sexual awareness flooding through her.

Holding her gaze, he knelt over her, one knee on either side of her slim body. 'You look as though you've never seen a man before,' Carlo mocked gently.

The blood sang in her veins as the soft touch of his legs against her thighs made her tremble. She could not tear her eyes away from his, all her naïve love and desire there for him to see. 'I haven't, not like you.' The words were a breathless whisper, as she raised her hands towards him in invitation.

Carlo lay one finger over her mouth, carefully tracing the outline of her soft lips; then, bending his head, his lips brushed gently across her eyes, the soft curve of her cheek, the tip of her nose, briefly teasing.

Helen's heart beat like a drum against her ribcage. She was sure he must hear it, but didn't care and, winding her arms around his neck, she pulled him closer, her lips parting in anticipation. His mouth covered hers, his tongue gently probing in a sensuous exploration, while one hand deftly untied her bikini top, swiftly removing it. Slowly he broke the kiss, leaning back to stare down at her near-naked form.

'You're beautiful, so beautiful,' Carlo declared huskily, his thumbs gently rubbing the rosy-tipped peaks into an aching rigidity.

Helen hardly heard his words as wave after wave of delight shuddered through her. A low groan escaped from deep in her throat as her body arched under him, her small hands feverishly gripping his broad shoulders.

His lips again closed over hers in a kiss of deep possession, and all rational thought left her as she was swept along on a tide of sensations only hinted at before. His strong hands caressed and cajoled, sweeping down over her stomach to find and remove the last barrier of her nakedness, but Helen was not aware of the fact. Then his mouth left hers, trailing a string of kisses down to where a pulse beat madly in her throat, and lower still, to the soft curve of her breast.

Carlo raised his head and, looking deep into her passion glazed eyes, he demanded, 'You will marry me, Helena. Promise me you will not let anything or anyone dissuade you.'

'Oh, I promise! I promise, Carlo, I promise,' she moaned, barely registering what he was asking, too achingly aware of every satin-skinned inch of him to want to talk.

Her eyes closed, as his tongue teased the fullness of her lips and then plunged deeply into the moist, dark cavern of her mouth. The blazing sun dazzled her heavy lids, but it was nothing in comparison to the blazing fire Carlo was creating inside her.

There wasn't an inch of her he didn't kiss or caress. His lips burnt a trail of fire down over her breast, his mouth sucking rapaciously on her turgid nipples, then lower. One strong hand teased her inner thighs, gently parting her legs, as his tongue licked in and around her navel.

Helen tensed, her eyes fluttering open, and Carlo's hand stilled on her thigh, sensing her resistance. Lifting his head, his dark eyes burnt into hers.

"I want to feel you, to taste you, Helena,' he groaned, his breathing heavy. 'Don't stop me now. Trust me,' he demanded. And she did...

Her eyes closed, her fingers tangling in the silky blackness of his hair, as his hands resumed their searching caresses. The blood flowed molten through her veins, unimaginable sensations coursing through her.

'Carlo,' she moaned, over and over, as deep shudders raged through her, her body convulsing uncontrollably, until eventually she lay trembling in his arms.

'You like that, *cara mia*?' he murmured throatily against her lips, his mouth claiming hers, gently as a whisper.

'Yes, oh yes,' she sighed. 'But should...'

'Hush,' he mouthed against her cheek. 'With lovers, anything is permissible.'

In one swift movement he turned on his back, carrying Helen with him, so that she lay spreadeagled on top of his hard body. She felt the slight shudder that ran through him, as he groaned, 'Now it is your turn, Helena. Touch me, know me...'

Helen needed no second bidding. She had no previous knowledge of a man's body, but her own burning desire for Carlo more than made up for any lack of experience. The husky male scent of him excited all her senses, his sweat-slicked skin tasted like nectar in her mouth. She exulted in the fierce pounding of his heart as she slid down the long length of him, her tongue flicking across his small male nipples, as her slender fingers traced the line of soft body hair leading to his briefs.

Carlo's hands entangled painfully in her long hair as he pulled her away from him, groaning, deep in his throat, '*Basta, basta*, enough!'

He gently eased himself upon one elbow, his breathing still erratic, a wry smile twisting his sensuous mouth. 'You emerald-eyed witch! Never in my wildest dreams did I imagine you could be so fantastically responsive. You make me feel like a randy sixteen-year-old,' he mocked, a rueful twinkle in his dark eyes. 'You are mine now,' he laughed, grinning down at her lovely flushed face. 'But right now, we had better cool off!' And in one swoop, Carlo lifted her in his arms and plunged them both into the pool. Much later, once again dressed in their swimsuits, they sat at the patio table and shared a bottle of wine.

That was how her father had found them. Even now, Helen shivered at the remembered anger in her father's voice.

'What the hell are you doing here, Manzitti?'

Carlo carefully placed his glass on the table and stood up, his voice soft, with an underlying hint of steel.

'Good evening, Mr Coulthard. It's been a long time.'

Helen sat, glass in hand, stunned by what she saw. It was glaringly obvious that the two men knew each other, but Carlo had never mentioned it. Her father stepped forward, his face a dull red, his eyes leaping violently with rage. While Carlo stood perfectly still, his hard, muscled body tense and wary, perfectly in control, his presence exuding absolute authority.

'I suggest we go inside, Mr Coulthard. I have an important matter I wish to discuss with you.'

Her father, nowhere near as controlled, bit out, 'There is nothing you have to say that would ever interest me, Manzitti, so I suggest you leave immediately, and stay away from my family.' He turned to Helen. 'Get in the house, girl. I'll deal with you later. This man is just leaving.'

At her father's words, Helen finally found her voice. 'But, Father, you don't understand! This is Carlo, a friend of Maria's. Why, he runs a marina with Roberto. You must be confusing him with someone else,' she ended, almost pleadingly, sure her father was making a terrible mistake.

Carlo put a hand on her shoulder. 'Leave this to me, Helena,' he murmured. 'Obviously, you are not about to listen to reason, Signor Coulthard,' he said hardily. 'I have asked your daughter to be my wife, and she has agreed. We would like your blessing but, if that is not to be, it makes no difference. I intend to take Helena to

Sicily on Sunday to meet my family, and we will be married in about three weeks. At eighteen, she does not need your consent.'

Helen watched a series of expressions flit across her father's face, from stunned amazement to raging anger.

'Over my dead body!' he shouted. 'Don't you know who this is? Why he is doing this, Helen?'

Then her father proceeded to tell her the whole sordid story. How, when her father and Maria had met and fallen in love, she had been engaged to Carlo. Her father, an honourable man, wished to tell Carlo, but Maria had been too frightened, with good cause, according to her sister-in-law, Caterina, who had confirmed her fears. She had been bulldozed into the engagement in the first place, and there was no way Carlo would let her break it. That was why they had fled to England while Carlo was away on business for a few days. They had been married at Caxton Hall by special license before Carlo found out.

As for him being part-owner of the boatyard, that was the smallest part of his business interests, just a handy place to berth his yacht. He was a millionaire many times over, his reputation as a playboy well earned. Notorious in Rome for his affairs with beautiful women, he ate little girls like Helen for breakfast. How could she be so foolish? As a Sicilian, the only reason he wanted Helen was revenge. Hadn't she heard of the Sicilians' adherence to the vendetta?

At her father's words, Helen found her shining confidence in Carlo's love turn to ice in her breast.

Carlo made no effort to deny anything, but just stood arrogant and aloof, as though listening to the enraged mutterings of an idiot. She turned to him, her eyes silently beseeching him to deny her father's words. He did not.

'I was engaged to Maria, that is true, but only because it was convenient for both of us at the time. I admit that I considered her marrying your father, without informing me, rather ill-mannered, but she has since explained the reason and I am satisfied it was unavoidable, given the circumstances at the time. Or, at least, she thought so,' he drawled sarcastically. 'And, yes, I do have other business interests. As for the rest, it is not worthy of comment.'

Helen stared long and hard into his dark eyes, wanting to trust him. Her father, sensing her hesitation, drove the final needle of doubt into her troubled mind, reminding her they had never returned to Sicily since his marriage simply because the all-powerful Manzitti family had made it impossible for him to do so. His permit to continue his excavation had been revoked, and six years of work had ended abruptly the year he had married.

Helen knew how much her father's work on the island had meant to him, and waited in an agony of doubt for Carlo to deny stopping it, but as she looked at him she knew he could not. For the first time, Carlo was hesitant in his reply. He denied it had been his doing, but was aware it had happened at his father's instigation.

She felt as though her heart had splintered into a thousand pieces at his words. Then anger had taken over, at herself mostly, for being so trusting, so foolish as to fall in love with a man like Carlo. She remembered her own outpourings of love, while he had only ever said he wanted her. He must have laughed himself silly at how easily he had won her girlish heart. She had taken a great gulp of wine, trying to steady her trembling limbs, determined not to break down in front of the two men.

Then Carlo had taken her arm, saying arrogantly to her father, 'This discussion is irrelevant. Helen has promised to marry me, and that is fact. I think, under the circumstances, it is better she come with me now.' He was almost dragging her from the chair as he spoke.

With stark clarity, she saw a picture of herself earlier that afternoon, lying lost in love in Carlo's arms, while he, nowhere near as affected, had insisted she reiterate her promise to marry him. And she had, over and over again, senseless with desire. The memory finally snapped the last thin thread of control she possessed and, leaping to her feet, she screamed at him, 'Let go of me! How could you? I hate you! Hate you...'

The rest was a blur. Fighting free of Carlo, she had run round the pool, her eyes blinded by tears, her father's voice, shouting her name, barely heard.

Maria found her at the bottom of the garden some hours later, and gently led her back to the house. There was no sign of Carlo, only her father's terse statement confirming for her that her romance was over.

'Mr Manzitti has driven back to town, Helen, and you will never have to see him again. It was just unfortunate that Maria had been too frightened to snub him in the first place, for then none of this would have happened.' He ended with a crisp order that Carlo's name would never be mentioned in their home again. Maria, rather shamefacedly, helped Helen to bed, saying it was all for the best, as Carlo was far too old for her, in any case.

Helen rolled over on to her stomach, burying her head in the pillow. Even now, two years later, the memory of Carlo's bitter betrayal of her young love still had the power to hurt.

On returning to England, she had taken up her place at university. Her father had insisted, but it had been a very hard time for her. She had changed overnight from a confident young girl, eager for life, to a reserved young woman. That one week with Carlo had awakened her, and she was horrified by her own wantonness.

At university, she was permanently wary of every male she met, terrified that perhaps she would behave as shamelessly again. The nights were even worse, as she lay in bed, unable to sleep, her body racked with longing, while her conscious mind fought a bitter battle with her seductive memory.

It had been the following spring before she'd made friends with anyone. Then Helen and Robbie had joined the sailing club, and gradually, over the summer months, she began to enjoy life again.

It was sad, but true, that the death of her father and Maria, so tragic, had finally cured her of thinking about Carlo. The grief she felt at their deaths, had taken up all her emotional capacity. There had been no question of going back to university in the September; she had to start earning a decent living as soon as possible. Her father had not been a wealthy man, and all the money he'd left was put in a trust fund for Andrea. His name was already down for his father's old public school, and Helen and her grandmother agreed that the young boy must have the education his father would have wished for him.

Helen had enrolled for a secretarial course at the local college, and had been pleasantly surprised at how much she enjoyed it. She'd begun to go out on the occasional date, and was relieved to find she had no trouble at all in fending off the more amorous suitors. The last couple of months, working at Garston's and earning her own living for the first time, had completed her metamorphosis into a confident young woman. Carlo's reappearance in her life this afternoon had dealt that confidence a severe blow.

Restlessly, she turned over on the bed. It was too incredible to believe he had gone to so much trouble to get her here. A wry smile curved her lips; but then, why not? It was no worse than what he had done last time. Tricking her, by his sexual expertise, into promising to marry him. He had wanted her body, there was no doubt in her mind about that. Without conceit, she knew she had the brand of looks the opposite sex found attractive. How lucky Carlo must have thought himself, to find the girl he intended marrying for revenge so attractive and so wantonly responsive to him. He had said as much. But love... the word wasn't in his vocabulary! Given the circumstances, she could have been as ugly as sin and he would still have gone ahead with his plan, but with a lot less enthusiasm.

Oddly, she had believed him when he said his engagement to Maria had been a mutual convenience. In Rome, Maria had not behaved as if at all embarrassed in his presence, as one would expect if they had been lovers. But Carlo was a proud man, so it could not have been easy for him to accept his fiancée running off and marrying someone else, especially as his engagement would have been public knowledge, here, in his homeland. The embarrassment to his family he would be unable to forgive, and her own defection must have really rubbed salt on the wound.

Her father had been correct in his assesssment of Carlo's motive for wanting to marry her, she had no doubt about that.

Carlo had told her, the very first day they had met, that a Sicilian male would not stand for being jilted, and she, poor fool, had thought how sensitive he was. She could see, now, it must have been one of the few times he had told her the truth.

With a snort of disgust, she swung her legs over the side of the bed and stood up. How false! Carlo was about as sensitive as a boa constrictor, and twice as deadly.

Swiftly she stripped off her bikini, walked into the bathroom, covered her hair with a plastic cap, and stepped into the shower. The stinging needle-spray went some way to soothing her overheated body, and the unpleasant memories flying around in her brain.

Briskly, she dried herself with the large, white, fluffy towel provided. Then, dropping it over the bath, she walked back into the bedroom. Her suitcases stood empty by the window; Sophia must have unpacked her clothes. Opening the first drawer of a large chest, she found her underwear. Crossing the room, she slid back the wardrobe door, and chose a simple cream dress, then slipped it over her head.

Helen grimaced at her reflection in the mirrored door.
The sleeveless dress plunged low at the front, revealing
the soft curve of her breast. The skirt clung gently to
her hips, ending just past her knees. She did not want
to give her gaoler any ideas, she thought, adjusting the
neckline slightly. Then, with a determined shrug, she
tightened the thin gold belt around her waist. Finding a
matching pair of gold sandals, she slipped them on her
feet, then crossed to the dressing-table to apply her make-
up.

She did not need any foundation; her skin was a
natural pale gold. Quickly she rubbed in some
moisturizer, then flicked her long lashes with a brown
mascara. A rose-pink lip-gloss for her lips and she was
ready. Her eyes lit with amusement at the picture she
presented, all dressed up with a plastic cap on her head.
Catching sight of the bedside clock, she saw it was
already after eight. Hastily she removed the cap, and
shook out her long hair. She brushed it vigorously,
clipping it back behind her ears with small gilt combs.

Straightening her shoulders, a sudden determination
strengthening her spine, she rose and left the room. She
would talk to Carlo now, before they went to his father's,
before he could get her any more involved in his life.
She would tell him she was leaving tomorrow, and that
was that. It was the nineteen-eighties, for heaven's sake,
not the eighteen-nineties! He couldn't get away with it.
He couldn't be serious about keeping her here; she had
a family, a home. He must see reason. As she descended
the stairs, however, the thought came unbidden to her
mind that, given his heritage and attitude to life, he
probably thought that what he intended was perfectly
reasonable. She walked through the double doors into
the *salone*, feeling rather less confident, but just as determined to have her say.

Carlo was leaning negligently against the fireplace, one
hand toying with a small porcelain figure on the mantelpiece, a crystal glass of what looked like whisky in the

other. He looked up at her entrance, his eyes raking her slender frame with a blatant sexual thoroughness that left her feeling as if he had stripped her naked.

Helen could feel a slow flush spreading through her body at his scrutiny and a feeling of helplessness overtaking her as she stared at him, huge and elegant, his dark jacket taut over his broad shoulders. She swallowed nervously, looking away. Why was it, of all the men she had ever met, he was the only one to have this effect on her? With a wry grimace, she sat down in the nearest chair.

Carlo's deep voice broke the lengthening silence. 'Early, Helena.' He glanced at a slim gold watch on his wrist. 'You surprise me. I fully expected to have to drag you from your room,' he mocked. Replacing the figurine on the mantelpiece, he crossed the room to join her.

'I'm glad to see you're going to be sensible. Can I take it you agree to my proposition?' he questioned silkily.

Helen lifted her head, his dark presence intimidating her. 'No, you cannot. I want to talk about that,' she demanded, somehow managing to sound much cooler than she felt.

He sprawled his large frame in the chair opposite, saying, 'Well, Helena, what did you want to say? I thought I made your position here perfectly clear this afternoon.'

'That's just it, Carlo,' she interrupted, taking a gulp of wine to steady her nerves. 'I know you hate my family, and perhaps you have some reason. Maria was a lovely person and it must have been hard for you when she married my father.' Not sure why the thought of Carlo and Maria should cause a twinge of pain in the region of her heart, she continued, 'But they are both dead, and the past is over, finished. Surely you can see that? I have Gran and Andrea to think of. There's no way I can stay here,' she pleaded. 'You must let me go home, if not tomorrow, then in two weeks, as Stephano arranged.' She did not want to mention her own involvement with Carlo two years ago, but she had to make him understand. In a low voice, not daring to look at him, she continued, 'Surely your taste for revenge must be satisfied by now? You made it impossible for my father to continue his work here. Then, in Rome...' She could not bring herself to speak about that period. 'Well, you know what happened. You can't possibly expect anything from me...' She tailed off.

Slowly she raised her head, hoping her words had convinced him of the futility in bringing her here. Her heart sank as she studied him. He was gazing down at his drink, idly twisting the glass between his long fingers, his expression hidden. For the first time since their meeting again, she noticed the changes in him. His face was much thinner than she remembered, the strong jaw more determined, the deep grooves from nose to mouth harsher, somehow. Her eyes fixed on the jagged V-shaped scar that slashed from the corner of his eye, across the temple, then at right angles over his high cheekbone. As she recalled his explanation for it, an unwanted feeling of guilt flooded her mind. Before, Carlo had appeared young for his age; now, with his black hair sprinkled with silver, he looked his years.

Bitterness was etched in his face as he caught her studying him. 'So, Helena, once again you want to run away, only now the circumstances are slightly different. This time you are in my home, with no doting father to help you.' An evil glint flashed in his dark eyes. 'You can consider yourself lucky to be here, and I am prepared to marry you. I could have arranged to get your stepbrother just as easily, and I am positive you wouldn't like that.'

Helen was stunned by his words. Marry her? After all that had happened between them, he must be mad. And, as for harming Andrea, he would not dare. But, as soon as the thought entered her head, it was negated.

This man would dare anything to get his own way...

She jumped to her feet. Flushed with anger, she stood trembling before him. 'You wouldn't dare touch Andrea. He's only a child!' Fear made her normally soft voice strident.

'Wouldn't I, Helena? Try me. After all, your father warned you how unscrupulous I am, and you believed him,' he drawled sarcastically.

'But you couldn't get away with it. It would be outright kidnap! You couldn't get him out of England, you'd end up in prison.' She could hear herself babbling, so horrified was she at the mere suggestion of any harm befalling her darling little brother. In that moment, she hated the man before her with a ferocity she hadn't realised she was capable of.

'Really, there is no need to be so melodramatic, *cara*. I have no intention of kidnapping your brother. Surely you credit me with more subtlety than that?' he derided.

Helen was puzzled. His harshly attractive face was bland, giving nothing away. He was a devious devil, that much was certain, but she could not imagine how else he could harm Andrea. Drawing a deep breath to bank down her rising panic, she said, 'I don't understand, then. How could you harm Andrea?'

'No, you don't understand. You never did.' For an instant, an expression she did not recognise flashed in the depths of his dark eyes and was gone. 'I have no intention of harming him. I believe he takes after his mother in looks, no trace of your fair-skinned father evident,' he murmured pensively. 'Also, he was born rather early after the wedding, only eight months, in fact.'

Helen tensed as he leaned forward in his chair, giving his words more emphasis.

'It would not take much to persuade a judge, for example, that the boy could as easily be mine as your father's. Maria was *my* fiancée until the day she left Sicily.'

Helen felt as if all the air had left her body in one breath, and her face paled beneath its tan. He meant it... She recognized instantly the cold, implacable determination in his voice. Still hoping she was wrong, she whispered, 'I don't believe it! How could you suggest such a thing?'

'Quite easily, *cara*,' he drawled, placing his glass on the table and standing up, towering over her threateningly. She was unable to check a hasty step back, angry at herself for allowing him to see she was afraid of him.

Smoothly, he continued, 'I would not have to prove the child was mine, only instigate the court action. The resultant publicity would be bad enough for the boy, and I doubt if you and your grandmother would enjoy it much, either. With a good lawyer, the case could last years, and take every cent you possess.'

'You're despicable!' Helen spat out, her hands clenching at her sides in frustration, itching to slap his arrogant face.

'You wouldn't dare,' he mocked, correctly reading the frustrated anger in her flashing eyes.

His amusement was like a red flag to a bull and, without considering the consequences, her arm shot out in an arc. But, before her hand could connect with its intended target, Helen found her wrists clamped firmly behind her back by one of Carlo's large hands.

In a voice thick with contempt, she snapped, 'I wouldn't have believed even you could sink so low as to threaten a child.'

Twisting sharply in his hold, she tried to break free of his grip, her slender thread of control snapping completely.

'Let go of me, you vile, arrogant pig!' she screamed, delivering him a sharp kick on his shin as she spoke.

His response was instant, as with one swift twist he pulled her hard against him. For long moments Carlo stared down at her flushed, mutinous face, his iron self-control evident in the tautness of his body, an ice-cold gleam in his eyes. 'Now, one more word…just one, and you will find out exactly how vile I can be. Understand?' he growled, and she did. 'We are going to my father's house, and you will behave as a loving *fidanzata* should.'

'Never!' she bit out, anger getting the better of her reason.

'You would rather I took your brother?' Not waiting for an answer, he continued, 'You promised to marry me two years ago, and now is pay-off time, Helena,' he informed her icily.

Finally she admitted to herself how expertly he had trapped her. He knew there was no way she would allow Andrea to be harmed. A low groan escaped her at the futility of trying to oppose him.

'Do I make myself clear?' he rasped, forcing her eyes to meet his.

She stared into their inky blackness, and wondered how she had been foolish enough to compare them to brown velvet. She nodded her head, all thought of fighting gone. She could not win. Her whispered, 'Yes' was barely audible.

Carlo gave a triumphant laugh. 'Excellent! I knew you would see it my way eventually.' And, letting go of her wrists, he stepped back, his hands closing gently on her waist.

Helen jerked convulsively, from fear or fervour, she was not sure. The only thought in her head to get away from him. 'You can take your hands off me now. You've got what you wanted. I agree to stay here, although I'll hate every minute of this charade of an engagement, but I want your promise you will not harm my brother, ever.' At least if she was going to pay him off with her body, she was going to make damn sure he wouldn't turn around later, when he was tired of her, and wreak his revenge on Andrea as well.

'There is no charade about it, Helena. In case you have forgotten, let me refresh your memory. We have been engaged for quite some time, and on Friday we will be married. As for your family, you have my promise, I will arrange for them to dance at our wedding,' he mocked cynically. Letting go of her, he casually drew a gold case from his jacket pocket, opened it, selected a small cigar, and lit it.

Helen was stupefied by his words. 'You mean, I have to *marry* you? But that's ridiculous! You can't be serious, we hate each other. I thought you only wanted to...' She ground to a halt, unable to put it into words.

'You thought I only wanted your body in my bed?' he queried silkily, drawing on the cigar, his narrowed eyes surveying her through the blue curl of smoke. 'Lovely as you are, I want more than a bed partner. That I can get anywhere. No, my dear, you are to be my obedient Sicilian wife, the mother of my son. Nothing less will do.'

She looked up at him through her thick lashes, her eyes drawn to the long, tanned finger idly rubbing the scar at his temple. But perhaps it was not so idle, perhaps it was a subtle reminder... She had imagined he wanted to humiliate her, take her to his bed till he tired of her, then throw her out. But now she realised his hatred went much deeper. He meant to force her to marry him, make her life one long humiliation; and the terrible part was, he could. She had no doubt he would try to take Andrea, but he was so well known he wouldn't have to. Presenting the case to court would give the Press copy for months. The notoriety would have no effect on him, for he was used to it, but it would destroy Gran and Andrea. God forbid, he might win. With Maria and her father dead, there was no one to gainsay him. Before she realised what she was saying, the words popped out. 'Just one question, Carlo, for my own peace of mind. Could Andrea be your child?' Immediately she regretted asking. How could she have thought such a thing?

Carlo laughed throatily. 'I wondered when you would get around to asking. Your trust in your own sex is about on a par with mine: non-existent. But let me reassure you, there is no way Andrea could be mine. My relationship with Maria was never that close.'

'My God! you really are a fiend. Is there anything you would not do to get your own way?' Helen asked, amazed by his admission, knowing somehow that it was true.

'Where you are concerned, no. And if that makes me a fiend, so be it. We have wasted enough time, my father hates unpunctuality. So what's it to be, Helena?' he demanded impatiently.

The anger he aroused in her faded, and she said dully, without further thought, 'Yes, I agree.' Her emotions had received too many shocks to assimilate in one day. Slowly, she turned towards the door. 'Shall we go? I would hate to add unpunctuality to all my other crimes,' she murmured, hardly knowing what she meant.

CHAPTER FOUR

HELEN sat in the passenger seat of the gleaming white Mercedes, head back, eyes closed. It was unbelievable that only yesterday she had been at home with Gran, busily packing, excited at the thought of a fortnight's working holiday in Sicily. Now, twenty-four hours later, she was driving through the night with this cynical, domineering male, on the way to meet her future father-in-law.

She found it too incredible to believe that Carlo still wanted to marry her, solely for revenge. In Rome, they had met by accident, and the opportunity to get even with her father, through her, must have seemed too good a chance to miss. But she would never have put him down as the sort of person who would sit plotting and planning for two years, and at great expense to himself. It must have cost a mint to buy out Garston's.

No, he was too much a man of the eighties, worldly and sophisticated, for his story to ring true. Anyway, with Maria and her father dead, whatever he did could not harm them. True, she had jilted him as well, but it was hardly the same thing. If her running away had really angered him, he was much more likely to have chased straight after her. But he hadn't bothered, obviously not that interested.

Helen's forehead creased in a frown. There must be more reason than vengeance. He had said he wanted a son; that she did believe. But why her? There must be millions of women who would jump at the chance of being his wife. What was it he'd said? 'An obedient Sicilian wife.' That must be it. With Helen safely incarcerated on the island as a glorified breeding machine, the swine could pursue his sybaritic life-style in the sure knowledge she would not dare object, where with any other woman, he would at least have to go through the motions of being an attentive, loving husband. Or perhaps, for some reason, he could not marry the woman he loved.

They travelled for some ten minutes or more in deafening silence, Helen's thoughts skidding helplessly between past and present. She could feel the tension building in the close confines of the car, like an invisible force-field, slowly sucking her in. They were travelling much faster now. The tires screeched as the car swung around a corner, flinging her across the seat, so she fell hard against Carlo's shoulder.

She straightened abruptly, 'Don't you think you're driving rather fast?' she snapped, flicking him a quick glance. The scar at his temple gleamed white in the reflected light of the headlights as he turned his head slightly.

'So you *can* speak! I was beginning to think you intended to spend the whole journey sulking,' he drawled sarcastically, ignoring the question, although the car slowed perceptibly.

She searched desperately for something to say, finally remembering the reason for their journey.

'Tell me, won't your father think it odd, your turning up with a fiancée he knows nothing about? How will you explain our meeting? What if he asks me questions? I can hardly tell him the truth, that you virtually kidnapped me!' Her voice rose in agitation at the thought of the evening ahead. 'I'm not much good at pretending.'

'Come now, Helena. You underestimate yourself. I remember you in Rome as an excellent little actress,' he derided.

'I don't know what you mean, and anyway...'

He interrupted her viciously, 'No...I don't suppose you do, and you care even less.'

Helen stared at him, surprised at his bitterly voiced comment. Resentment burnt in her veins. If anyone had been acting in Rome, it was him, she thought grimly. Hadn't he pretended to be in love with her, let her make a complete fool of herself, all for some weird lover's revenge he imagined he was entitled to?

'Nothing to say, Helena? What's the matter, don't you like to be reminded what a very enthusiastic lover you were?' A humourless smile twisted his lips as he continued, 'Until your father decided otherwise for you, that is.'

There was enough truth in his statement to make argument impossible so, with a nonchalance she did not feel, Helen replied, 'The past is of no interest to me. I don't have your capacity for revenge. All I want to know is what I am supposed to say to your family to get me through the evening with the least possible aggravation. I've had just about enough for one day,' she ended sullenly.

His dark head turned towards her, studying her intently for long moments in silence. Then he turned his attention back to the road. 'You have nothing to worry about. My father knows the truth. He is a Sicilian of the old school, and considers it perfectly natural you should marry me. It resolves his notion of the vendetta perfectly,' he intoned blandly. 'As for the rest of my family and friends, they believe we met when I was in England in June, acquiring Garston's Advertising, and renewed an old acquaintance with you. Stephano, of course, knows the truth, but can be trusted to keep quiet.'

It hurt that Stephano knew the whole story, and was instrumental in bringing her to Sicily. She had considered him a friend. Obviously, being two years older had given her no more sense where men were concerned. She had been just as easily fooled a second time, only now there was no one to help her out of the mess she found herself in.

Reading her thoughts correctly, Carlo continued, 'The wedding will take place on Friday at the chapel on my father's estate. In the evening, there will be a reception at the Hilton in Palermo for my friends and business associates. And this time there will be no running away,' he opined hardily.

'I didn't run away!' she burst out. 'You know what happened. Though, discovering the truth about you, I would have gone anyway. And as soon as I get the chance I will leave here,' she added vehemently. 'You won't be able to watch me all the time.' She was still not quite prepared to submit absolutely to his plans. A bark of derisory laughter met her comment.

'I don't need to, *cara*. You can't leave the island without my knowing, and you wouldn't get far without a passport.'

Stephano! She had given him her passport on arrival, completely forgetting to ask him to return it when they had cleared Customs. A low groan escaped her at the helplessness of her situation. 'I suppose you have my passport?'

'You suppose correct. Stephano handed it over, along with your delectable self. So I suggest you forget any wild ideas of escape.'

The car drew to a halt, and Helen looked around interestedly. They were parked in the courtyard of a large house, lights pouring from a dozen windows in the magnificent facade, reflected in the waters of a large ornamental fountain in the centre of the yard.

As she reached for the doorhandle, Carlo caught her hand. She flinched at his touch.

'Wait!' he said sharply. Reaching into the inside pocket of his jacket, he withdrew something. 'Give me your other hand.'

'Why?' Helen demanded bluntly.

'You cannot meet my family without this.' She looked at him in stunned silence as he slipped a magnificent emerald and diamond ring on the appropriate finger. Her breath caught in her throat as she recognised it, and she could not prevent her hand trembling in his, or exclaiming, 'It's the same ring!' Her eyes flew to his face questioningly.

'Why not? It is the one you chose, though it has taken quite a lot longer than originally envisaged to get it on your finger,' he gibed, dropping her hand and getting out of the car.

Helen stared dazedly at the ring on her finger, tears moistened her eyes as she remembered their choosing it together. Fleetingly, she wondered if perhaps her life would have been happier if her father had never told her the truth. Fearfully, she pushed the thought aside, instinctively aware such ideas were dangerous in her present situation. It would be all too easy to fall under this man's spell for a second time.

Carlo's hand grabbed her arm, almost dragging her out of the car. 'You're cold,' he remarked, his arm coming around her back, his long fingers curving on her bare shoulder. 'You should have worn a wrap, the evenings can be cool.'

Helen made no comment, all her energies concentrated on staying calm, so she never saw the look of tender concern in the dark eyes of the man holding her. She carefully eased herself away from his hold on the pretence of looking around. The hall was wide, panelled from floor to ceiling in a dark wood. Doors opened off either side, and in the centre a massive carved staircase curved to the upper floors. Old oil paintings adorned the walls, mostly portraits, as far as she could tell, and bearing an uncanny likeness to the man beside her. She stared around her in amazement; the place was like some medieval castle.

A voice spoke from behind her in rapid Italian. 'Carlo! How good to see you.' Helen turned in time to see Carlo embracing a small, grey-haired lady, dressed in the obligatory black.

'Rosa, you look younger than ever,' he said, holding the slight form away from him and smiling broadly, a grin of genuine pleasure lighting his harsh features, making him appear years younger.

Helen nervously accepted the effusive congratulations bestowed by the smiling woman, who she gathered was the housekeeper.

They followed Rosa into the room on the left, and Carlo kept a tight hold on her arm. Bending his head as they entered, he whispered, 'Just remember to be polite to my family.' And, before she realised what he intended, his lips brushed softly against hers. The gentle caress caught her off guard, and her own lips parted involuntarily under his. Realising her spontaneous reaction, she turned her head, blushing a fiery red.

Carlo's triumphantly whispered, 'Don't be embarrassed, *cara*, sexual chemistry rarely changes,' had her wishing she could slap the smug grin off his face. She was furious for responding to his kiss, and was just about to make a scathing retort when she realised they were standing in front of an old man seated in a motorised wheelchair.

Helen quickly masked her surprise. Carlo had said his father was not well, but she had not thought to find him in a wheelchair. Carlo introduced her, moving around to the side of his father's chair, as he did so.

She would have known without being told that this was his father. There was no mistaking the likeness, almost a mirror image, except this man's hair was white. The face was the same, harsh and arrogant, but with many more lines, the flesh hanging loose on the bones. Even seated, it was obvious he had been a very large man. Her eyes flew to Carlo leaning casually against the side of the chair. He looked straight at her as his father spoke.

'You're late, Carlo. You know how I hate unpunctuality.' Carlo did not answer immediately, but blatantly allowed his eyes to roam over the girl standing before him, noting the golden hair floating loosely over her shoulders, the curve of her breasts visible through the cream silk of her dress, then lower, down to her hips and long shapely legs.

'Don't you think Helena is a good enough reason for any man being late, Father?' he returned, as his gaze slid back up her body.

She felt as though he had stripped her naked with his studied appraisal, and could not prevent the colour rising in her face. The two men laughed together, delighted at her embarrassment, his father replying, 'This time you can be forgiven, son. She really is quite exquisite!'

Helen stiffened at his words, furious. They were discussing her as though she was some beast at auction, but she refused to be ruffled. 'Thank you, Signor Manzitti.' Smiling sweetly, she added sarcastically, 'You are too kind.'

The old man's eyes sparkled wickedly in his ravaged face. 'She has spirit, this one, Carlo. You have chosen well. You will make fine sons together.'

'We fully intend to, don't we, Helena?' Carlo challenged, looking straight at Helen, amused at the fury dancing in her eyes, and daring her to disagree. She was about to do just that, ready to tell them both exactly what she thought of them, when he moved slowly towards her, taking hold of her wrist, his fingers like a manacle. All amusement was gone as he stood towering over her like some predatory animal. His dark eyes narrowed to slits. 'Don't we, Helena?' he repeated, his voice low and deadly.

She held his gaze for long moments, flushed and angry. Then, lowering her head, she murmured, 'Yes, Carlo.'

The old man cackled his delight, not at all put out by his son's show of strength. 'That's right, boy. Let her know who's boss.'

Carlo ignored his father's comment, watching Helen's downbent head with a glimmer of tender compassion on his face, quickly blanked out, as he said, 'We had better go in to dinner, Father, you're frightening Helen. She's not yet used to outspoken Sicilian males.'

They walked through large double doors to the dining-room, Carlo holding them for his father to go first and seating him at the head of the table, then holding out a chair for Helen on his father's left, and taking the seat opposite for himself. Helen sat down thankfully. At the back of her mind had been a vague idea of throwing herself on the mercy of some kind old man who would be appalled by his son's behaviour, and help her get home. After meeting Carlo's father, she had no such illusions. If anything, he was worse than his son. He would have done the same thing himself, without waiting half so long, she conceded wryly.

Pulling herself together, she looked around the room. The dining-table was huge and beautifully set, the fine silver cutlery and crystal glasses set off to perfection by the immaculate white linen. A lovely centrepiece of red rosebuds and freesia in a silver holder, added the finishing touch.

Rosa entered, pushing a large hostess trolley, closely followed by another woman, who was introduced by the old man as his daughter, Simonetta, as she sat down next to Helen. She was a very lovely lady, dressed all in black. Helen surmised that she must be a widow, then recognition struck. She was the image of Stephano; obviously this was his mother and, as she looked nothing like Carlo, she guessed that she must take after their dead mother. Her speculations halted as Rosa served the first course, a delicious minestrone soup, so thick the spoon almost stood up in it.

The conversation revolved around the wedding and the arrangements to be made, with lots of light-hearted banter that Helen was finding harder and harder to take, so it was with relief that she finally rose from the table and followed the others into the lounge.

Her head was beginning to ache, and she was quite desperately tired. Moments after being seated, she had to hide her surprise as Carlo sank his powerful frame on the sofa next to her, far too close for comfort. The slight spicy tang of his cologne teased her nostrils and she dared do nothing about the arm he placed around her shoulders. Her whole body tingled at his touch. With fear, she told herself adamantly.

'You won't mind if we leave?'

Helen dimly registered the words and heaved a sigh of relief. The evening was finally coming to an end.

Carlo rose and held out his hand to her, saying with an expression of rare tenderness lighting his features, 'Come on, my darling, you're falling asleep. It's been a long day for you.' For a moment she was fooled by his care, and put her hand in his, allowing him to pull her to her feet. His hand slid down around her waist, holding her to his side. She relaxed against him. She really *was* exhausted, the food and wine she had consumed, slowing her reactions. His father and Simonetta followed them to the door and as Helen breathed the fresh night air she revived slightly, stiffening in Carlo's hold. He had done it again, tricked her into submission, for his family's benefit, she thought rebelliously.

'Not as bad as you expected?' Carlo queried.

Helen glanced across at the man seated behind the wheel, unable to gauge his expression fully in the car's dim interior. 'Simonetta is very nice. I liked her.'

'My father not so much, hmmm? Why not? He adored you. You made quite a hit with them all, your nervousness adding just the right touch for a girl meeting her future family for the first time. I congratulate you. The evening went very well.'

'Thanks to you,' Helen snapped sarcastically. 'Do you always manipulate people, even your own family?' She realised Carlo had cleverly guided the conversation all evening, deftly fielding any awkward questions, sidetracking Simonetta when she had asked about Helen's family, and who were to be the witnesses at the wedding, informing his sister that they were lunching tomorrow with friends of his who had agreed to stand for them.

'Don't thank me, darling,' he derided. 'I did it for myself. I don't want you suffering from nervous exhaustion on our wedding night.'

There was no answer to that. The mention of their wedding night filled her with dread, the thought of this man possessing her too frightening to contemplate. She slid lower in the seat, twisting the ring on her finger in agitation. God, what a mess!

In her girlish dreams of her wedding day, she had seen herself floating down the aisle on her father's arm, radiantly happy to marry some kind, gentle person. All her family and friends would be there to wish her luck... But that could never be now. Who would have thought that two years could make such drastic changes in a girl's life? Tears of self-pity clouded her eyes. Angrily, she brushed them, away with the back of her hand. She would not give him the satisfaction of seeing her cry.

Forcing herself to speak normally, she asked, 'Who is to play the part of my father at this wedding?' Remembering that Maria's brother lived in Sicily, she answered her own question. 'Roberto, I presume? He *is* a friend of yours.' She had been a bit hurt that he had not attended Maria's funeral, but still, she continued, 'It would be quite appropriate, after all, he is my only living male relative old enough,' she ended wryly.

The car swerved and ground to a halt at the roadside.

'Don't you know?' Carlo demanded roughly, swivelling in his seat to glare at her, his mouth twisted in an ugly smile.

'Know what?' she asked warily, wondering why they had stopped.

'He is dead. He died the week before Maria.'

Helen gasped in horror, one hand fluttering to her mouth and down again. 'Oh, no! No, Carlo, I can't believe it. He was so young, so full of life.'

Carlo stared hard at the beautiful face turned towards him, the shock and horror registered there, genuine even to his cynical mind. 'Either you're the greatest actress ever, or you really did not know. I wonder which?'

'Truly, I had no idea.' In a voice thick with emotion she murmured, 'There must have been a funeral, but Maria never left home.' Accusingly, she demanded, 'Did you tell her, in time for her to attend?' She wouldn't put it past him to have delayed informing them, simply to be vindictive.

'Oh, I told her, all right. She knew exactly what happened. He was lost at sea. A storm blew up when he was out sailing. They recovered the boat, but never found the body. It is why you were not told that intrigues me. Your father must have been more afraid of me than I thought.'

'My father was never afraid of anyone in his life, and certainly not you,' Helen defended stoutly, adding, 'I was probably not at home at the time or something.' Her voice tailed off, and she lowered her eyes to hide her own uncertainty. Privately, she wondered why she had not been told. After Rome, her father's edict that no mention of the trip would be allowed surely couldn't have extended to Roberto as well. Her thoughts turned inwards; she sighed, recognising that it was probably her own fault. She had been so determined to block the whole episode out of her mind that she had never talked to Maria about her brother. The one time she had met him was the night Carlo had proposed to her, and it was too painful a memory.

Carlo's hand curved around her shoulder, pulling her towards him and, taking her chin between her finger and thumb, he forced her face up to his. The atmosphere in the car subtly changed, a new tension in the air. Helen was trapped by the dark intensity of his gaze, unable to break the contact. It was as if he could read her every thought.

'Remembering, aren't you, *cara*?' he drawled seductively, his hand dropping from her face to linger teasingly across the top of her breast. 'I have such vivid memories of a beautiful young girl, who melted in my arms, whose lips caressed my body in wanton abandon, who promised to be my wife.'

Helen shuddered in his arms, her face suffused with colour, unable to deny the truth of his words. His head bent lower as his hand moved to cup her full breast. She had to stop him before she did exactly what he had reminded her of, and melted in his arms again. Already she could feel the tiny flame curling in the pit of her stomach. With a supreme effort of control, she knocked his hand away and blurted, 'The only thing I need to remember is that my father told me the truth about you. You were engaged to Maria, and your ego couldn't take her leaving you to marry my father. You deliberately set out to persuade me to marry you, solely for revenge. And you can't deny it,' she ended on a sharply indrawn breath.

Ignoring her outburst, Carlo's lips and moist tongue licked softly over her mouth. He raised his head, his husky, cynical laugh humiliating to her ears.

'As I recall, you were more than willing to be persuaded.' Then he added, fully aware of her attempt to hide how he affected her, 'And soon will be again.'

Helen lifted her hands to his chest to push him away, but he caught her wrists, his dark eyes icing over and, in a voice as brittle as glass, continued, 'I was engaged to Maria once, in that your father was correct. As for the rest, I did not think it warranted an explanation, but then I did not know how possessive your father was and how much he hated my family until that night.'

Helen stared at his handsome face through a haze of tears. Her soft lips trembled, as the emotions she had fought so valiantly all day finally overwhelmed her. Tears sparkled on her long lashes like raindrops in the sun, then fell fast and furious down her cheeks, her slim body shaking with the sobbing she could not control.

Carlo gently pulled her into his arms, cradling the back of her head in his palm, holding her tenderly against the warmth of his broad chest. 'Hush, Helena, it's all right. I didn't mean to upset you. Don't cry, please, don't cry,' he whispered soothingly against the top of her silken head.

But she was past hearing, as she gave in to a storm of weeping, for Roberto, Maria, her father and, perhaps most of all, herself.

Slowly Helen regained some control of her shattered emotions. Carlo's strong hand stroking her hair, the warmth of his body enfolding her, comforted her as nothing else could. The fact that he was her enemy she forgot for the moment as, hiccuping on a sob, she buried her head in his chest, content. All her fears vanished in the safe haven of his arms, and for a while he was the old Carlo, tender, sensitive, as he had been the day they had first met, so long ago.

Later, she was unaware of the large man removing his jacket and, lifting her sleeping form, carefully tucked it around her, or of the soft kiss brushed lightly over her mouth.

The car sped silently through the night, a tender smile curving the driver's lips.

CHAPTER FIVE

HELEN slowly opened her eyes; the early morning sun shone through the window, bathing the room in a golden glow. She turned sleepily to the clock on the bedside table. Seven... She lifted one hand to her mouth, yawning hugely, then froze. Her hand dropped to her breast as the events of the previous day spun through her mind like a film run at high speed, and in the same instant she realised she was naked under the thin cotton cover. Carlo must have put her to bed. She could remember nothing after breaking down and sobbing her heart out in his arms. Her cheeks burnt at the thought, and with a sigh she rolled over on her stomach, burying her face in the pillow.

She thought of Gran and Andrea, and knew, with a numbing certainty, that he would do exactly as he had threatened, unless she agreed to his demands.

Didn't it say in the Bible somewhere that the sins of the father were visited on the children? She had never really believed that, but her first experience with Carlo had literally proved it. He had been determined to make her pay for her father's supposed insult, and now... What of her own defection?

Looking back, she knew it had been fear as much as anger that had made her run away from Carlo but, even more than that, shame. Shame at her own behaviour, the wanton girl she had become in his arms. In retrospect, she could see it had been the humiliation, the blow to her self-respect, that had hurt most. Carlo had deliberately, cruelly exposed the sensuous side of her nature, never restraining her ardent caresses, but delighting in them, as he had led her along the path of eroticism. And she had been such an eager pupil, that learning the true reason for his action had nearly destroyed her.

Well, this time he would not find it so easy, Helen vowed to herself. She was older, and a lot wiser now. She accepted that, short of a miracle, the wedding would take place, but she had one or two demands of her own to make, whether he liked it or not. The acceptance of her immediate future eased some of the turmoil in her tired mind, and gradually she drifted back to sleep.

Helen woke to hear the sound of china rattling. A glance at the clock revealed that it was after eleven, and she sat up, pushing her tumbled hair from her face, to see Sophia entering the room, carrying a tray bearing a large coffee-pot, and a cup and saucer. Remembering her lack of night attire, she hastily tucked the bedcover under her arms, as Sophia walked across to the bedside.

'*Buon giorno*, *signorina*, you slept well. It is almost noon, and I have brought your breakfast,' Sophia said, smiling happily.

'*Buon giorno*, Sophia. I'm sorry it's so late, you should have called me earlier,' Helen responded apologetically, speaking in Italian without conscious thought. 'I'll have my coffee on the terrace, please. Oh, and *focaccia*, my favourite!' she exclaimed, noting the dimpled savoury bread alongside a large bowl.

'*Si*, *signorina*, the *patrono* insisted. He tells me you have a great passion for it.' Turning, Sophia walked out on to the terrace. Helen leapt up, and grabbed her towelling robe from the bottom of the bed. Wriggling into it, she tied the belt tightly around her waist, hoping Sophia had not noticed she was naked, then followed her on to the terrace. Fancy Carlo remembering she liked *focaccia*! She had tasted it for the first time years ago, as a child on her first visit to Sicily, and loved the taste of the savoury bread dipped in a bowl of milky coffee. Years later, in one of those rambling conversations lovers share, Carlo had asked her what she liked best in Italy, and she had answered, teasingly, *'Focaccia.'* He had reached out and grabbed her, and they had ended up kissing.

Hastily, she pushed the memory from her mind. For some reason, it disturbed her. She did not like him, and she was under no illusions as to how he felt about her, he had made it very plain. She was someone to be used; to provide a son and heir for the Manzitti family, at the same time satisfying his burning desire for a thwarted lover's revenge. She did not want to think of him as being in the least considerate. So it was rather abruptly she thanked Sophia, and told her to go.

Immediately she regretted her sharpness, as the smile left Sophia's face.

'*Si, signorina.* The *patrono* said to tell you to be ready at twelve.'

Helen forced herself to smile brightly at the older woman, not wanting to upset her. 'Thank you, Sophia. I will be,' she said kindly, and was rewarded by another glimpse of Sophia's amazing false teeth as she left, slightly mollified.

Hungrily she tucked into the food, telling herself that one never won a war on an empty stomach. With a sigh, not quite of contentment, more of resignation, Helen stood up to look out across the bay. The rocks rose out of the sea at each end of the beach, silent sentinels, enclosing the villa and surrounds in an aura of isolation.

Well, if she was to be Carlo's captive wife, he could hardly have chosen a more beautiful place to imprison her! The vague feeling of familiarity she had experienced on arrival was still with her. Then it hit her. Of course, the last time she'd been here, with her father, they had visited a friend of his on the bay of Castellammare. While the men talked, Helen had gone to explore. She had walked for a long time and had been very hot. Stripping off her clothes, she had swum naked in the sea around a headland, and found this beach. She had spent some time here, thinking she was alone, then she had seen a man, and been terrified, shooting back the way she had come. What a coincidence, all these years later, Carlo building a house in the same cove. Perhaps he had been the stranger that day. With a shake of her head, she turned impatiently and went back indoors. Really, she was becoming too fanciful for words!

Quickly she showered and slipped on a brief green bikini with a matching halter-necked sundress. If the people they were to visit were like Carlo, they would probably have a pool, so she would be prepared. She brushed her long hair and tied it back with a green satin ribbon; a touch of waterproof mascara to her lashes and a pale lip-gloss for her mouth and she was ready.

Helen settled on a lounger on the patio with the morning paper, glad to find she was on her own. Sophia had said they were to leave at twelve, and it was that time already, but she wasn't about to go and look for Carlo. The less time she had to spend in his company, the better she liked it.

A prickling feeling in the back of her neck warned her of Carlo's presence. Glancing up from her newspaper, she saw him leaning casually against the doorframe of the *salone*. He was dressed formally in a dark three-piece suit that moulded his large frame to perfection. His hand tugged off the tie at his throat as he approached.

Undoing the top few buttons of his silk shirt, he spoke. 'You slept well, I trust, and now you are waiting for me. How flattering!' he mocked sardonically, reaching out and running a long finger down her cheek.

Helen flinched, and dropped the paper on the table. 'Sophia said we were going out at twelve and, like your father, I dislike unpunctuality,' she stated, not averse to some sarcasm of her own.

Anger flashed in his dark eyes, but was quickly masked. 'You have decided to be sensible, and behave as an obedient fiancée should,' he opined, ignoring her quip.

'If by that you mean will I give into your blackmail and marry you, the answer is yes, as you knew it would be. I won't have you harming Andrea, and I know from experience what a ruthless swine you are.'

'You know me so well, *cara*,' he drawled suggestively, holding her gaze, sensuous amusement dancing in the depths of his eyes. 'Every inch, in fact.'

Helen jumped to her feet, flushing scarlet at his implication. 'I know you well enough to realise you would do what you threatened,' she qualified.

'Good, then we are agreed. Now, if you will excuse me, I must get changed.' His fingers deftly unfastened his waistcoat, then shrugging off his jacket, he continued, 'It's too damn hot for this rig-out.' He turned to go.

Helen found herself watching him dazedly. His shirt, damp with sweat, clung to his muscular torso, his trousers fitted trimly over hard buttocks and long, long legs. At six feet four, he really was a magnificent male animal.

'No, wait!' Helen blurted, finally remembering her earlier decision to talk to him. 'I want to discuss...'

Carlo didn't stop, but called out dismissively, 'Not now, or we will be late.'

Helen's eyes widened in anger. He didn't give a damn that she had agreed to his proposal, so supremely confident was he that she would. He might have shown some pleasure at her acceptance, she thought, then shoved the idea to the back of her mind unwilling to pursue the implication. How she would love to dent that hard male ego, and anger at her own impotency toughened her resolve.

'Carlo, I am going nowhere with you until you hear what I have to say. I have a couple of demands of my own and, if you don't accept them, you can do your worst.' She only just stopped herself from adding childishly, 'So there!' It gave her great satisfaction to see her words had stopped him in his tracks, but when he spun round and walked back to her, it took all the courage she possessed to stand her ground. His cool indifference was gone.

'So! Are you threatening me, Helena?' he asked, in a voice dripping with ice. His strong hands snaked out, grasping her shoulders. Her skin burned where he touched her, but she refused to be cowed by his harshly voiced comment.

'I don't want to argue with you, but I will have my say.'

'Well, well, you would try to defy me, hmmm?' Carlo's hands slackened on her shoulders as he studied the defiant flush on her lovely face. 'You are different this morning. Yesterday you were terrified. I wonder what has brought about the change? Dare I say it, you have decided to behave like an adult, perhaps?' His tone belied his belief in his own conclusion.

'Perhaps I have grown up in the last twenty-four hours.'

Letting go of her, Carlo turned back to the house, murmuring, 'I wish I could believe that.'

If Helen had not been so wound up in her own emotions she might have wondered at his comment, or noticed the dispirited droop of his broad shoulders. Instead she demanded, 'Are you going to listen to me, Carlo?'

'Yes, if I have to. You can talk while I change.'

'I'm not coming upstairs with you.'

'Don't be ridiculous. What do you think I am going to do? Leap on you as soon as you're in my room?' He turned, one brow arched mockingly. 'I thought you said you were adult, for God's sake. I am going to change *now*. If you want to talk, you know where to find me,' he bit out, exasperation evident in his voice as he turned and walked quickly into the house.

Slowly she followed him upstairs to his room. He was right, she *was* being childish.

'Pour me a whisky. It's over there.' He indicated a cabinet by the window. 'I will have a shower and be with you in a minute.'

'Should you be drinking so early in the day? It can't be good for you.' I sound like a nagging wife, she thought irrelevantly, walking across to the cabinet.

'I need it,' he replied, going through an open door at the side of the room into what Helen presumed must be the bathroom.

Helen breathed a sigh of relief as he disappeared. What did he mean, he needed a drink? When she knew him before he'd drunk very little: the occasional glass of wine or champagne. He certainly wasn't a whisky drinker. For a fleeting moment she wondered if he was as nervous as she was, then grimaced at her own foolishness. The man was pure steel, through and through, without a nervous bone in his body. Pouring a large measure of spirit into a crystal glass, she left it on the cabinet, and turned her attention to the room.

Her own bedroom was lovely, but this was fantastic. The same arched windows led out on to the terrace, but that was the only similarity. It was much larger, and decorated in a deep cream and maroon. The intricate plaster mouldings on the walls and ceiling were picked out in gold. A cream carpet covered the floor, and maroon drapes, trimmed in gold, hung at the windows. But it was the bed that caused her to gasp in amazement. It was a huge, ornately carved and canopied four-poster, the drapes and cover a matching maroon colour, beautifully embroidered in gold silk. Obviously antique, more in keeping with a sultan's harem than a villa in Sicily. Yet somehow it fitted the room exactly. She could just imagine Carlo lounging on the pillows like some eastern potentate.

"When you have finished admiring our bed, perhaps you could enlighten me as to what is so important that it could get you into our bedroom.'

Helen looked up, startled, to see Carlo picking up the glass of whisky. His hair, damp from the shower, curled on his forehead. He had changed into a pair of slim-fitting brown trousers, and a short-sleeved cream sports-shirt. No man had any right to look so good, she thought. Then, realising what he had said, 'What do you mean, our bed?'

'This is the master suite, the dressing-room opens off the bathroom. I have been using it up until now. Unfortunately I haven't had time to see about the rest of the place, as you probably noticed. Still, furnishing the villa will give you an interest until the children arrive,' he ended, laughing at the stunned expression on her face.

'I haven't seen over the villa yet. You mean to say, it isn't finished?' Helen queried, diverted for the moment.

'Oh, the building is complete, but you caught me on the hop a bit with the rest of it. I didn't intend to bring you here until November.'

'You didn't what?' she cried. 'Then why am I here now?'

Carlo's lips twisted in a cynical smile. 'Oh, that's easy! Stephano informed me you were spending the weekend with some man, Robbie. Though I am quite determined to marry you, unlike your family I would prefer not to force you to break an engagement, which could easily have followed, after spending the weekend with your boyfriend. Any man who once knew you would not easily give you up,' he opined hardily.

Helen looked up at him in angry amazement. 'But... but that's rubbish!' she stammered in her haste to get the words out. 'Do you mean to say that if I hadn't mentioned going sailing for the weekend to Stephano, I wouldn't be here at all?' she asked incredulously.

'Yes, that is correct,' Carlo replied, amused at her confusion.

'Of all the ridiculous... Robbie's a girl!' she shouted, furious that such a simple mistake could be the cause of getting her into such a mess. 'Short for Roberta! We joined the Thames Valley Sailing Club in the spring. That's where we were going for the weekend.'

A wide grin split Carlo's face, and he laughed out loud. 'Don't look so furious, Helena. I'm going to have you in any case. The only difference is that we will have to wait until November for our honeymoon. I can't get away just now.' His dark eyes gleamed with mock sympathy. 'I'm sorry about the delay, but I'm sure you understand.'

There was, perhaps, no difference to him, but there certainly was to Helen. By November, anything could have happened. She was so enraged, she itched to knock the self-satisfied smirk from his handsome face, and without a second thought, shouted, 'With luck, you could have been dead by then!'

She succeeded better than she could have imagined for Carlo's lips narrowed to a tight line. For a second, she thought she saw a flicker of pain in his eyes, as he turned and walked to the dresser, saying sarcastically, 'It's nice to know your true opinion, *cara*.' Picking up a comb, he raked it through his unruly black hair, adding grimly, 'Dare I turn my back on you, I wonder?'

Helen was swamped with shame. It had been a rotten thing to say. Much as she disliked him, she would not have wished him any physical harm. Hesitantly she crossed to where he stood and, lifting a hand, tentatively touched his broad back. 'I'm sorry, Carlo. I didn't mean what I said.'

He stiffened at her touch, his eyes locking on to hers through the dresser mirror. Then gradually he relaxed, his lips quirking in a smile. 'No, maybe you didn't, but I think we had better get to the reason you came to my room in the first place, or we'll never make it to Aldo's.'

She sighed with relief at his words. The last few minutes had made her forget the determination she had felt this morning, but now he had reminded her, and quickly she broke into her speech. 'First, Andrea. He goes to school in September, so won't miss me too much, but I insist on spending all the school holidays with him, either at home or here. Gran is very fit, but can't be expected to do everything herself——' She hesitated, her hand falling from his back as he turned around to face her. She was not quite sure how to phrase her second condition.

Carlo arched one dark brow enquiringly. 'There is more?'

'Yes.' Then, in a rush, she got the words out. 'Once I have your child, I want my freedom. You have to let me go.' Bending her head, she nervously ran her damp hands over her hips, as Carlo stood watching her. She could feel the force of his gaze through her scalp, so intently was he studying her.

'Let me see if I have understood correctly. You will spend all your holidays with your family. Well, I can agree to that. I am a great believer in families. After all, that is why I am marrying you,' he drawled cynically. 'As for the rest... Your freedom after the birth of our child...' Briskly, he caught her chin in one hand, turning her face up towards him.

Helen tensed as his thumb carelessly rubbed her chin, a slow warmth building in her body. Fiercely, she stamped on the rising tide of feeling his touch evoked. This time, she would not back down.

Carlo looked deep into the soft green eyes which were bravely trying to defy him, his own expression impossible to read. 'You are still as impulsive as ever, Helena. Do you not know yourself any better, even after two years?'

She didn't understand what he meant, and she wasn't about to ask. 'I am not interested in discussing my character, Carlo. Just give me a straight answer. Do you agree?'

'You mean, to go, leaving the child here with me?'

'Yes, that's right.'

His hand dropped from her face as she spoke and, swinging around towards the door, he said, 'Okay, I agree, if that's what you want.'

A gasp escaped Helen at his words. She couldn't believe it had been so easy. She'd had a whole list of arguments ready. Following him out of the room, she murmured a 'thank you'. He took her arm and led her downstairs, and she could not hide the note of triumph in her voice as she added, 'I am glad we understand each other, Carlo.'

He cryptically stated, 'Oh, I understand you, Helena. It is whether you understand yourself, that will be the problem!'

Elated at having won the concessions she had asked for, Helen was disposed to be pleasant as they drove up the tree-lined drive from the house. The building really was exquisite. In the midday sun, it shone like a jewel suspended on the hillside.

'It's a lovely villa, Carlo. Does it have a name?'

'No, not yet. I rather like the sound of "The Villa Helena".' He spared her a smiling glance, before asking smoothly, 'Do you approve?'

Helen was loath to break the tenuous truce they appeared to have established. This morning there had been little trace of Carlo's bitter anger of yesterday, and she wanted it to stay that way, so diplomatically she replied, 'Of the house, yes.' She ignored his quip about the name. 'Who designed it?' she queried, hoping to divert him.

'I did.'

Helen spun round in her seat. '*You* did!' Surprise was evident in her voice. 'I didn't know you were an architect. I thought high finance was your field.'

'There is a lot you don't know about me, but then we never had much time for talking before,' he mused. 'I seem to remember you preferred other, more active, pursuits, Helena *cara*.'

Her determination to remain pleasant melted like ice in a fire at his mockingly drawled comment. 'I'd prefer not to be reminded of the past.'

She was fed up of his Italian alteration of her name, it brought back memories she had fought hard to forget. 'And my name is Helen, not Helena,' she declared adamantly.

Carlo made no response, only shooting her a sardonic glance before returning his attention to the road negotiating the powerful car through the Sunday traffic with visible expertise.

She was surprised to see that they were driving through the resort town of Mondello. Somehow, she had gained the impression that his friends lived in the country. Breaking the lengthening silence, she asked, 'Do your friends live here?'

Watching the crowds of people strolling along the sea front, she couldn't imagine this being Carlo's cup of tea, or that of his friends.

'No, they live inland, about another ten minutes.'

Helen shuffled uneasily in her seat. The thought of having to meet yet more strangers was not at all inviting. She couldn't help asking, rather worriedly, 'What are they like? Have you known them long? Do they know about me?'

His firm lips tilted at the corners, in the beginnings of a smile. 'Very nice. Aldo, all my life, Anna, his wife, the ten years they've been married, his three children, all their lives, and yes.'

It took Helen some while to work out what he had just said, and she wasn't much happier when she had.

'Won't they be surprised at your producing a fiancée out of the blue, especially as they know you so well.'

'Not at all. They are very good friends, and wouldn't dream of questioning me. But you will do nothing to make them think this engagement is anything other than a love match,' he warned hardily. 'It shouldn't be too hard for you to convince them. All women are great deceivers,' he ended with sardonic cynicism.

Helen didn't deign to reply, but turned her attention to the passing scenery. The car slowed to negotiate a particularly sharp bend, and Carlo afforded her a swift glance, saying, 'I have asked Aldo to design the wedding rings. He has a jewellery shop in Palermo, but his main occupation is the design and crafting of jewellery.'

Helen sniffed; tossing her head, she allowed her gaze to slide over the man beside her. Did he think she was in the least interested in what sort of ring he put on her finger? In the circumstances, it meant nothing, anyway. But Carlo wasn't about to let her get away with so much as a derisory glance.

'You will endeavour to be suitably enthusiastic. Am I making myself clear?' he demanded, as he swung the car into a concealed entrance and up a long drive, to stop in front of a large house.

'Yes, Carlo, I understand,' she sighed, instantly recognising the underlying threat in his words.

Unfastening his seat-belt, he turned towards her, the expression in his dark eyes amused and faintly mocking. One long finger reached and gently traced the outline of her mouth. 'You have beautiful lips, *cara*,' he husked sensuously, then laughed out loud at the look of astonishment on her face.

Helen turned bright red, and it was a flushed and embarrassed girl that slid out of the car. Carlo was still grinning as he closed the car door and, taking her arm, led her up the steps to the main door. For a moment, she glimpsed the man she had known, but the tiny pain that curled through her stomach she dismissed as hunger; they were late in arriving for lunch.

Carlo's hand moved from her arm to her shoulder, as the door opened and their hosts appeared. Helen stiffened, trying to ease away from him, the touch of his thigh brushing lightly against her was doing disturbing things to her equilibrium. Sensing her resistance, Carlo tightened his fingers on the bare flesh of her shoulders as he made the introductions, apologising for their late arrival, explaining he had been detained at church. So that was where he had been this morning, so formally dressed. Helen flicked a cautious glance through her lashes at his harshly attractive face, surprised. He did not strike her as a religious man. More in tune with the devil, she would have said.

Aldo was a typical Sicilian, not much taller than Helen, with black curly hair and brown eyes, and about the same age as Carlo, while his wife, Anna, looked a few years younger. She reminded Helen of Mary in the office at home. Small and plump, with curly brown hair and bright blue eyes, she was not beautiful, but her friendly smile was captivating. Helen liked her on sight, but wished the circumstances of their meeting could have been different.

Anna led them through to the rear of the house and out on to the patio. Helen had made the right choice in clothes; there was a sparkling oval swimming pool, and past that a rather dried-out lawn with the odd tree here and there, obviously a place for the children to play, rather than a formal garden.

The three children were a delight: Cesare, Marco, and Selina, aged nine, seven, and five respectively. They were all excited at seeing their Uncle Carlo, and Helen was amazed at the change in him, as he swung the little girl up high in his arms, planting a swift kiss on her soft cheek. The harsh lines disappeared from his face, his dark eyes gleaming with rare tenderness. It was obvious that he adored her. Anna told her later that Carlo was godfather to all the children.

CHAPTER SIX

AFTER lunch, the men were dragged off to the bottom of the garden to play football with the two boys. Anna suggested Helen strip to her bikini and stretch out on a lounger, while she put the little girl to bed.

Her hostess returned within minutes and lay down on the adjacent lounger, explaining that Selina had been ill for some time, but they hoped she was recovering now, though she still tired easily. It had been a great worry to them, but Carlo had been marvellous lending them his apartment in Rome while Selina saw the specialist there. It was obvious Anna considered Carlo a great friend, and very compassionate man. Listening to her extolling his many virtues, saying how kind and supportive he was, Helen couldn't help wondering how one man could appear so totally different. To Anna and her family, a valued friend. To Helen and *her* family, the complete opposite.

Luckily, Anna was a compulsive talker, and was quite content with just the occasional comment from Helen. It was only when she mentioned Carlo having once been engaged to Maria that Helen became slightly wary, wondering if perhaps the girl had her suspicions regarding the real reason for the marriage.

She was quickly reassured as Anna continued, 'It was just a convenience, of course. It was that sister-in-law of Maria's who was responsible, Caterina. You've probably met her, Roberto's wife—well, widow now.'

'No, I don't think I have,' Helen murmured.

'Perhaps it's just as well. She's a twenty-two-carat bitch! When she first came here, about eight years ago, she set her cap at Carlo, but he wasn't interested so she married his best friend Roberto instead. That's when the trouble started.'

'The trouble?' Helen interjected questioningly, intrigued by this insight into Carlo's past.

'Yes, Caterina was determined to split up the friendship between the three of them, and with Maria living with them it was easy. The sly comment, how Carlo was always visiting the house, and it must be more than friendship... but she was hoist by her own petard in the end. When Carlo got wind of the gossip, he silenced it by getting engaged to Maria. Caterina was furious, and went all out to cause more trouble. It was she who persuaded your father to run away with Maria, and Maria, being the timid creature she was, and hopelessly in love with your father, agreed it was the only way. Yet she knew very well that Carlo would not have objected to her breaking the engagement. In fact, he would have been the first one to wish her happiness, for she was like a sister to him. It was very naughty of Maria, and it made the Manzitti family look foolish; not that Carlo minded, but his father was livid.'

Helen was fast becoming confused at all this inside information, and wondered if she would ever know the true story. Added to that was a niggling idea at the back of her mind. 'Caterina... is that Caterina Belgosa you are talking about?'

'Yes, that's right. So you *do* know her?'

'Well, I think so. I've just connected the name with Roberto. Stephano introduced me to her last week, at a reception in London. She took an immediate dislike to me. In fact, she was downright rude.'

'That sounds like her. She can't stand women, so I wouldn't take it personally. But, if she knew about you and Carlo, she would make it more obvious. Take my advice and steer clear of her. She's trouble.' Anna grinned mischievously at Helen. 'I probably shouldn't have said that. Aldo is always telling me I talk too much, but forewarned is forearmed, I reckon.'

'That sounds dangerous!' Helen laughed, her gaze straying to the bottom of the garden, attracted by the noise the boys were making. At least, that was the excuse she gave herself.

Aldo and the children were crazily chasing the ball, while Carlo leant negligently against the trunk of an old olive tree, supposedly keeping goal, but obviously taking a breather. Turning his head, he caught her watching him, and immediately straightened up, smiling ruefully, aware she had seen him resting.

Stripped to the waist, with his dark hair ruffled, he didn't look much older than the boys, she thought, smiling back, her green eyes lit with amusement.

Calling something to the others, Carlo made his way back up the garden, Aldo and the boys trailing along behind him.

Seeing Carlo casual and relaxed, it was hard for Helen to believe all the things her father had said about him. Could Anna be right? she wondered. Was her version of his first engagement the correct one? Could her own father have been wrong? Immediately she felt guilty for doubting her father. Anyway, it didn't make much difference who was right. She was here now, and committed to staying. If Carlo had not loved Maria, and she was coming to believe it more and more, then why was he so angry? Helen pondered. Her own desertion could not have mattered to him, unless he had liked her for herself.

She watched him approach, unaware of the sensuous gleam in her lovely eyes. He moved with a lithe grace unusual in such a tall man, his muscular physique a joy to behold. She could see the tiny beads of perspiration, glistening like diamonds on the soft hair of his chest. Her tongue licked over her lips in an unconscious gesture. She could almost taste him, and her body flooded with heat at her wayward thoughts, until Carlo's voice shocked her back to the present.

'You look as though you have never seen a man before,' he mocked reminiscently, recognising the look in her eyes.

Helen blushed from head to toe, vividly reminded of the last time he had said the exact same words to her. 'Carlo, the boys,' she spluttered.

Leaning over her, an arm either side of her chair, he spoke so only she could hear. 'Wrong reply, Helena, but I will forgive you this time.' He kissed the tip of her nose affectionately, then added in a softer tone, 'Swimming pools and you are inextricably linked in my mind for all time.'

Before she could respond, Cesare shouted disgustedly, 'Uncle Carlo, I hope you aren't going all soft now you're getting married.'

'Certainly not!' Carlo replied, devilment lurking in his dark eyes as he swept Helen up into his arms.

'Come on, lazybones! It's time you got your bikini wet.'

She flung her arms around his neck, screaming, 'No! No!' But, with the two boys roaring encouragement, he dropped her in the pool. She hit the water with a resounding splash and went straight to the bottom. She surfaced, spluttering and choking, to see that Anna had suffered the same fate, and all the males were standing at the edge of the pool, laughing.

Eventually everyone was in the water, and for the next hour they all took part in a boisterous game of water polo.

Later, when they were all dried and dressed again, Anna went to wake little Selina, while Aldo took Helen and Carlo to his studio. He was delighted to show Helen around, explaining how he designed and fashioned jewellery, showing her some he had completed for an exhibition he was giving in Paris, New York and Sydney. She had not realised he was so well known, but should have guessed; the security was second only to Fort Knox!

One emerald necklace was particularly magnificent. The stones were set in white gold, and surrounded by diamonds to form a collar effect. Aldo insisted she try it on, then turned to Carlo.

'Perfect, my friend. Don't you agree?'

Carlo looked up from some designs he was studying, his glance flicked over the necklace, then much more slowly travelled on, as he studied every inch of the girl wearing it. Helen's face turned pink in embarrassment; standing with the fabulous jewels round her throat, she felt like some slave girl awaiting her master's approval. Her body tensed as though he had touched her, and it seemed an age before Carlo answered, though in reality it was only a moment.

'If anything can be perfect, that is,' he opined.

She looked up, and was trapped by the glitter of naked desire she saw in the depths of his eyes. A flash of awareness shot through her, frightening in its intensity.

Her fingers found the clasp of the necklace, and she removed it hastily. Her thoughts were thrown into chaos. However much Carlo hated her, however cynical his reason for marrying, on a purely physical level he wanted her badly. She knew it with absolute certainty. Would she really be able to share a bed with such a virile man for months, then walk away unscathed? The decision of the morning no longer seemed quite so easy, or such a victory. Mentally, she shook herself; as long as she remembered it was a cold-blooded coupling to appease his bitter desire for revenge, she would survive.

Aldo, having replaced the necklace in its velvet case, held out a set of rings, and speedily found Helen's size. After that, it was easy. Carlo had a very definite idea of what he wanted; three bands of gold, woven into a braid effect. All she had to do was agree, which she did, not in the least interested, as she had no intention of wearing it for long.

But she gasped in amazement when, to Aldo's query as to whether there was any particular significance in the design, Carlo replied quite seriously, 'Yes, Helena was wearing her hair in a braid when we were introduced.'

She flicked him a sidelong glance, puzzled. Was he mocking, or what? She would never understand this man in a million years, but with luck, she need not stay with him even one year. And on this happy thought, she followed Carlo back outside, while Aldo secured the studio behind them.

The rest of the afternoon passed pleasantly as they all sat around the pool, talking, with the occasional drink to oil the wheels of conversation. Selina was fascinated by Helen's hair, never having seen any that colour before, and insisted on calling Helen *'la donna d'oro'*, much to everyone's amusement.

She was a lovely little girl, though it was obvious she had been ill; considering she was the same age as Andrea, she was only half his size. Her skin was almost translucent, the veins showing blue in her small arms. Helen wondered what the child had suffered from, but was too polite to ask. It was clear the child doted on Carlo and, by the tender expression in his eyes as the child curled up contentedly in his lap, he obviously returned her affection.

Helen suffered one awkward moment when Selina, with the bluntness of the very young, asked if she could be bridesmaid at the wedding, and wear a long dress, saying with childish frankness that she had never had a long dress before. Helen was struck dumb, not knowing how to answer. She imagined the wedding would be a brief affair, with herself wearing a simple dress or suit, but she did not want to disappoint the child. Carlo came to the rescue, informing Selina she could certainly be a bridesmaid, and made arrangements there and then for Anna and the child to meet Helen the next day to choose the dress.

They finally left at about seven, after firmly refusing Anna's pressing invitation to stay for dinner.

Helen sank thankfully into the car seat, unexpectedly tired; the strain of playing the happy *fidanzata* had been more exhausting than she had imagined. She chanced a quick look at her companion, as he slid into the driving seat and started the car, with a last wave to the family in the doorway.

Once again, she wondered how he could be so brutal to her, and yet so warm and tolerant to his friends. Surely he must see, having spent so much time with a happy family, what he was sentencing them to by his insistence on this loveless marriage. To want to bring a child into the world, knowingly without love, was barbaric. She was about to challenge him, then changed her mind, noting the knuckles of his strong hands, gleaming almost white as he gripped the wheel, his long muscular legs, so close to her own, stiff with tension. Something was bothering him, and she did not have the strength or the desire to start another argument, so, turning her head, she looked sightlessly out of the window until they stopped outside the villa.

Helen followed Carlo's tall figure into the hall. She hesitated as he stopped at the door of his study, turning to wait for her. Slowly, she walked towards him.

'I'm tired, Carlo. What do you want now?' she snapped.

'I thought you might like to call your grandmother with our news. You can use the phone in my study.' Still holding her wrist, Carlo led her into the room.

Helen had forgotten all about Gran in the turmoil of the last couple of days, but he was right, she would have to ring and tell her something. What to say, however, completely defeated her.

'I don't know what to tell her. She's hardly likely to believe I have fallen madly in love in two days and want to get married.'

'Why not stick to the truth as much as possible, or is that too simple for you?' he derided, leading her over to the desk and, picking up a slip of paper, handing it to her, finally letting go of her wrist as he did so.

Helen stared at him mutinously, but was the first to drop her gaze, unable to stand the cynicism in his eyes, as he drawled, 'I also will speak to her, to clear up any points you may miss, Helena.' He was certainly letting her know he would stand no prevarication.

Looking at the paper in her hand, she was surprised to see it was her home phone number, with the appropriate code number added. Why surprised? Finding her home phone number was a simple thing, considering all the other arrangements he had made to get her here. Picking up the phone, she dialled the number.

Hearing Gran's voice brought a lump to her throat, and her eyes misted over with tears. Only Carlo's hand, gently covering hers, gave her back some composure. She refused to let him see how upset she was, and managed to ask after Andrea without a trace of emotion, flicking Carlo a bitter look as she spoke. That brought an answering derisory gleam to his eyes, and he mouthed silently, 'Carry on, you're doing fine.'

Oddly enough, his hand on hers, and the closeness of his huge frame, gave her the confidence to convince Gran quite easily. She simply told her that by an amazing coincidence Stephano's uncle, whose villa they were staying at, turned out to be a man she had met in Rome two years ago, and dated quite a lot. They had had to part when Helen had returned home to go to university, but now they were reunited and wanted to marry. Gran was delighted, if a little worried, when Carlo, by the expedient of a loud stage whisper, asked to speak. Reluctantly Helen handed him the phone, and stepped back a few paces to lean against the side of the desk, as Carlo introduced himself.

It was with a growing sense of frustrated anger that she listened to him. He was charm itself, as he explained how fond he had been of Helen two years ago, but had thought she was too young for a serious relationship.

Now, the age thing did not seem so great, and he was honoured that Helen had agreed to become his wife. And, of course, they would all have to meet before the wedding. He then proceeded to inform Gran that Stephano would be arriving in England on Wednesday, and would escort Andrea and Gran to Sicily the following day. Helen's mouth dropped open in amazement; he was so plausible, it was unbelievable! When he eventually handed the phone back to her, she found that all that was required was an occasional yes or no, as the older woman waffled on about how wonderful it was.

Helen had never realised before that her grandmother was such a romantic, and it was a relief to finally say goodbye and replace the receiver, numbly accepting that Carlo had triumphed again. He had seated himself behind the desk in a large leather swivel chair, his dark head bent over some papers before him. She looked at him dispassionately, wondering if the person had been born who could best him. His black hair, liberally sprinkled with grey, was longer than he used to wear it, and curled gently over the collar of his shirt. She might as well not have been there; he was already completely involved in his work.

Anger bubbled up inside her at the ease with which he had arranged everything to his advantage. A dozen choice comments ran through her mind, none of them flattering, but before she got around to voicing them he looked up from his papers and caught her watching him.

His firm lips twisted in irritation and, in a voice icily polite, he asked, 'Was there something else? I do have rather a lot of work to do.'

'My God! I don't believe it. How can you sit there so calmly after what you've just done?'

'I thought I did rather well,' he retorted, leaning back in his chair. 'Your grandmother appeared to be quite happy with the situation, and that is what you wanted. After all, the reason you are marrying me is to safeguard her and your darling brother, and I think I convinced her of your future happiness, perfectly,' he opined smoothly.

'You may have convinced her that we are wildly in love, but you overstepped the mark, inviting her here. She will realise in half an hour that there is something wrong. She knows me far too well, I could never hope to fool her. Why? Why did you do it?' Agitation at the mere idea of her grandmother and Andrea coming to Sicily was enough to make her voice rise an octave.

'Let's say your family are a kind of insurance policy, hmmm?'

'I don't follow you. Insurance policy?'

'But of course, *mia cara*. When you stand in church on Friday, the fact that your brother is just behind you will give you the incentive to say "Yes" as nothing else could.'

Helen gasped in horrified acknowledgement of his words. He was right, damn him! Knowing Andrea was here, on this man's property, was an insurance policy with a vengeance. Her green eyes flashed stormily at his duplicity, but one look at his implacable features was enough to stop the angry retort in her throat and, with a choked cry, she turned and fled, his mocking laughter ringing in her ears.

It was no good, she was not going to sleep any more tonight. The few hours she *had* managed had been haunted by visions of a dark, scar-faced man pursuing her, and she had awakened, burning hot, with the sheet twisted in knots around her slim body.

The first glimmer of dawn lightened the room as Helen left her bed and quickly slipped on her bikini. 'To hell with it,' she thought. The villa was silent so, taking a large towel from the bathroom, she quietly opened her bedroom door, and crept downstairs. In a matter of moments, she was outside. There was no one to see her run lightly down the terraces, and through the open gates to the beach. Only Gran and Andrea were staying at the villa, as Carlo, true to tradition, was spending the night before the wedding at his father's house.

Her wedding morning... She dropped the towel on the smooth sand and ran unhesitatingly into the cool arms of the sea. The turquoise water wrapped around her burning flesh in a cooling balm. She struck out determinedly, her mind numb. Only when she felt an aching tiredness in her limbs did she turn gracefully on to her back, allowing the soothing waves to hold her gently in their sway.

She had swum out further than she had realised, and the last hundred yards back to the beach were a struggle. It was with relief that she felt the sandy bottom beneath her feet, and staggered back up the beach, to collapse flat on her back on the sand.

She stared up at the heavens. The first rays of the morning sun were turning the few fluffy streams of cloud rosy-red. What was the rhyme? 'Red sky in the morning, shepherd's warning?' Her mouth twisted in a wry smile, it certainly was not a weather warning here! The last week had been blisteringly hot, and already the temperature must be in the seventies. Perhaps it was a more prophetic warning, that the months ahead were going to be stormy for *her*.

As Helen's breathing slowly returned to normal, so her thoughts calmed. The last few days had not been too bad. On the Monday, Carlo had driven her into Palermo to meet Anna and Selina, depositing the three of them at a very smart boutique solely for bridal wear, and, after some discussion with the owner, Carlo had left, informing them he would return in an hour to take them all to lunch. Helen had not cared what sort of dress she bought, so Selina was allowed to pick her bridesmaid's dress first, then Helen simply took the wedding dress it was meant to accompany. The light in the little girl's eyes as she had surveyed herself in the mirror was a pleasure in itself. The dresses were identical: frothy confections in tulle, with bows. A gently scooped neckline that could be worn on or off the shoulder, an empire-line bodice, trimmed with ribbon, and the same ribbon trimming the short puffy sleeves with small bows. Two hats, large and floppy with matching broader ribbons that floated down the back, completed the outfits, along with dainty satin shoes.

Selina looked positively ethereal, with the soft full skirt floating around her tiny feet. Helen smiled reminiscently. At least one little girl was going to be very happy today!

That day set the tone for the rest of the week. Carlo had returned at eight in the evening, and they had dined together like polite strangers, the conversational highlights being 'Pass the salt' or 'More wine?' After the meal, Carlo had retired to his study, leaving Helen to her own devices.

The rest of the days followed the same pattern. Helen made a point of not going down for breakfast until she was sure he had left for his office in Palermo. If he realised she was deliberately keeping out of his way, he had made no comment, so it obviously didn't bother him. He treated her with a cool politeness, and she was quite happy for things to remain that way,. He had made no effort to touch her, and if on the odd occasion she had caught a glimpse of the bitter anger he had shown on first meeting her again, she ignored it.

Helen's days were spent sunbathing by the pool, or swimming in the sea. The place was idyllic for a lazy holiday, and by Thursday the confidence she had felt on Sunday, when she had persuaded Carlo to agree to her terms for the marriage, was sky-high. Being married would not be so bad, she told herself. After all, she need hardly see him and, if she fell pregnant quickly, she would not even have to share a bed with him for more than a couple of weeks.

Unfortunately, last night that feeling of well-being had taken a hard knock, when Stephano had arrived with Gran and Andrea. It had taken every ounce of will-power

Helen possessed to stop herself from bursting into tears and telling her grandmother the whole story. But Carlo's presence had stopped her. One look at his face had been enough to convince her that he knew what she had in mind, and the warning was explicit in his dark eyes.

He and Stephano, between them had completely monopolised the conversation over dinner, and Helen had no chance to speak to her grandmother before Carlo was insisting they retire early, ready for the big day tomorrow. His excuse was that he had a long drive to his father's house for the night.

Helen could not avoid walking out to the car with him, nor could she avoid the kiss he planted on her unwilling lips. That was when the fear returned to haunt her. His arms closed like steel clamps around her, and his hard mouth covered her own. She stiffened in rejection, but he was much too skilful a lover to be deterred, and did not release her until the blood was pounding in her veins and her lips had parted, willing, under his. Then, with a mocking laugh, he had set her free, whispering, 'Just a reminder for tomorrow night, *cara*.'

Gran's voice calling her brought her back to the present, and she stood up, brushing off the sand that clung to her smooth skin as she watched the older woman approach. Gran made a pleasant picture in a light blue dress. She was tall, like Helen, but with grey hair and twinkling blue eyes.

'I thought I would find you here, darling. It's time you were getting ready. It will take at least two hours to wash and dry your hair.'

Helen looked at the gentle, smiling face before her, and a lump rose in her throat. 'I was just coming, I didn't sleep too well, so I took a swim to try and relax,' she said softly.

'It's bridal nerves, nothing to worry about. I remember when I married your grandfather I was just the same, but you will be fine. Carlo is a wonderful man. You are very lucky.'

A loving arm curved around Helen's shoulder and, forcing herself not to give way to the emotions choking her, she responded, 'Yes... Yes, I know I am.'

'What's the matter, Helen? Are you sure you want to get married?' Gran questioned, fixing Helen with an enquiring look. 'If you are at all doubtful, now is the time to say so, before it is too late.' The older woman was far too observant not to notice Helen's distress.

If only she knew, Helen thought sadly. It had been too late, the minute she'd stepped on the plane to come to Sicily. She ignored the question, and replied with one of her own. 'Tell me, Gran, when I am married would you like Andrea to come and live in Sicily with me?'

'So that's the trouble! I rather thought it might have something to do with your young brother. I know you, Helen, you want to take the responsibility for Andrea on your shoulders. But, my dear, it won't do. Since your father died, Andrea has become doubly precious to me. Taking care of him eases the pain of my loss, and it would break my heart to part with him now. After all, I am only just in my sixties, not so decrepit that I can't look after one small boy. And in another five years he will be in boarding school.' A sigh of acceptance escaped Helen, as her gran continued, 'If you're worried about the lack of male influence in his life, don't be. I meant to tell you earlier, but Joe and Martha are moving in with us. They are going to have the top floor, and you know how Andrea dotes on them both. Joe is like a second father to him. It would be cruel to take him away from his home now, when he has settled down again after losing his parents. So you see, dear, you have nothing to worry about. You and Carlo can start married life on your own, as it should be.' And, with a light laugh, she added, 'And I hope I will be a great-grandmother before too long!'

The news that Joe and Martha were moving into her old home sealed it, as far as Helen was concerned. For years they had rented the stables at the back of the house, using them for a pottery. Many was the happy hour Helen had spent watching Joe at the potter's wheel, creating beautiful objects with consummate ease. They had no children of their own, and were past the age to have any. She could not have wished for better people to be sharing Andrea's upbringing, but couldn't help feeling a little depressed to realise she was no longer considered essential in her own home.

'It isn't just Andrea, something else is bothering you?' Gran suggested gently.

Helen tried to laugh. 'No, not really. Only you have rather taken the wind out of my sails. I had all the arguments prepared to convince you I was doing the right thing, getting married so quickly, and it's a bit of a surprise to find I don't need them. You've accepted my marriage to Carlo so readily. I thought . . .' And she suddenly realised what she had thought. Ever since last Sunday, when Carlo had told her that her grandmother was coming, subconsciously she had been depending on her gran to object to the hasty marriage and insist on their waiting a while, knowing Carlo would not be able to argue with the older woman. But last night that last futile hope had gone and, with it, all Helen's confidence. In one last attempt, she said, 'Well, I can't help wondering what my father would have said.'

'Oh, Helen, darling, it's obvious Carlo loves you deeply, and he has waited two years already. I'm not blind, you know. When you came back from Rome, I knew there was something wrong. You lost weight, were silent, morose—all the classic symptoms of an unhappy love affair. I asked your father what had happened and he closed up like a clam. The only thing he would admit was that you'd had a girlish infatuation with a totally unsuitable man, but once you got to university and concentrated on your career, it would all be forgotten. I wasn't so sure, but didn't like to interfere. We Coulthards have all married young. I was eighteen when I married your grandfather, and your father was only twenty-one when he took the plunge. That's what caused the problem.'

'The problem?' Helen queried, not following her gran at all.

'You always did see your father through rose-coloured spectacles, but he was human like the rest of us, with very human feelings. In your father's case, it was an obsessive overprotectiveness. Now, I don't know if your father would have approved of your marriage, but I do know you have nothing to feel guilty about. Perhaps it will help you to understand if I . . .'

'There is no need, Gran,' Helen interrupted quickly. She had a sinking feeling she did not want to know any more; she did not like her gran's view of her father, was amazed by it.

'Perhaps not, but it is time you knew the truth.' And, sitting down on the sand, she indicated to Helen to join her. 'You never knew your mother, but she was a lovely girl. Your father was twenty, and in his second year at university, when they met. Helga was eighteen and working as an au pair in Cambridge. She burst into your father's life like a rocket. He was completely captivated, and within two weeks he dropped out of university, and the pair of them set off on the hippy trail to India. Nothing your grandfather or I said could stop them. It was the sixties—flower power, "children of light", they called themselves—and Helga was one of the brightest stars, almost too bright,' Gran murmured reflectively.

'Well, nine months later they were back and Helga was very pregnant. Your grandfather insisted they got married, he actually bought the wedding licence, but that was their only concession to a conventional life-style. You were not born at home, as you thought, but at a derelict farmhouse in the middle of Wales, the commune they were living in at the time. The birth was normal, but Helga died of peritonitis a week later. When they finally realised there was something wrong and took her into the hospital, it was too late. Your father told me later that the doctor in the hospital had been furious at the waste of such a young life, and as good as accused him of criminal negligence.'

'Oh, no!' Helen whispered, horrified at her gran's revelations.

'After that, your father was a changed man. He went back to university, then concentrated on his career. His whole life revolved around his work and you. For years he blamed himself for Helga's death. Unfortunately, it had the effect of making him determined you would not grow up like her. He was terrified you would marry young, without a career, or the opportunity to mature properly. That was why he kept you with him all the time, insisted you went to a girls' convent school, even though we aren't Catholic. And I hate to say it, but I think half the reason he married Maria was because she was such the exact opposite to Helga. Quiet and old-fashioned, almost, in her outlook. He actually told me he thought she would be a good influence on a young teenager like yourself.'

'Oh, Gran, surely not?' Helen cried, unable to assimilate what her Gran had told her.

'Don't misunderstand, Helen. He loved Maria, but in a different way from your mother, a better way, I think. They suited each other perfectly, much more than your mother and he did. So you see, Helen, when I said I don't know if your father would approve, I meant, given his outlook he may not. But I do know he would want you to be happy, and I am sure Carlo is the man to do that.' Looking Helen straight in the eye, she asked, 'You do love him?'

What could she say? All Gran had told her spun around in her brain; she knew later it would cause her deep concern, but now Gran was waiting for her answer, and what could she say, but 'yes'?

Whatever else was true, one fact still remained. Carlo was blackmailing her into marrying him, and Gran must never guess.

'I knew you did, darling. Now, come on, let's get back to the house and get you ready.'

CHAPTER SEVEN

THE small chapel looked beautiful with masses of flowers banked along the walls, the perfume almost cloying in the midday heat. Helen wondered idly when the church had last seen a wedding—probably Simonetta's. After her grandmother's conversation this morning, a fatalistic resignation had overtaken her senses, and it enabled her to sail through the wedding ceremony without a qualm.

There were only the immediate families and estate workers present, but the tiny church appeared full to overflowing. As Carlo slipped the gold braided ring on her finger, and she returned the gesture, she looked up at his cold, arrogant features and for a second she imagined she saw tenderness in his eyes, but was quickly disabused of the notion. A bitterly triumphant smile twisted his lips as he bent his head to drop a cool kiss on her brow.

They left the church arm in arm, the congratulations of the whole congregation ringing in their ears.

Carlo was at his elegant best, in full formal dress, including a top hat, while Helen was quite unaware of how lovely she looked: every man's fantasy, in oceans of floating tulle, with her golden hair streaming down her back. The cameras flashed incessantly; everyone present was determined to have their own personal picture of the occasion, as well as the official photographer.

At his father's house she was introduced to every last one of the guests, so that by the end of it the polite smile she had adopted felt glued into place.

The meal was excellent, and the best champagne flowed like water. There was no doubt it was a great celebration, the marriage of the son of the house. Carlo's father looked pleased with himself, and drank so much that Helen had a fleeting vision of him falling out of his wheelchair drunk, and smiled at the thought.

Carlo played his part of the loving bridegroom to perfection, never leaving her side. If she had not known differently she might almost have believed his caring looks, and the gentle touch of his hand on her shoulder.

Hour followed hour, and she was beginning to think the afternoon would never end. So it was with relief that she allowed Carlo to help her into the bridal car. A kiss for her young brother and Gran, who were leaving that night, a last wave to the assembled throng, then Tommaso was driving them away.

Her relief was short-lived, as she remembered there was the reception in Palermo to get through yet. Some two hundred friends and associates of the Manzitti family were gathered at the Palermo Hilton, waiting for their turn to toast the happy couple.

When she had queried the necessity for the second reception, Carlo had answered briskly, 'My father's ill health precludes him from attending large functions, but the Manzitti name is well known on the island, and a large reception is expected. Too many people would be insulted if not called upon to take part in the celebrations.'

The tension began to build up inside Helen as they sped along the main route into Palermo. She raised a hand to her head and removed the large hat, the rice caught in the brim covering Carlo as she did so.

'Throwing things at me already, *cara*!' he drawled cynically. 'I hope that's not an omen of what to expect later!'

Helen's stomach knotted in pain at his words, the reminder of their wedding night sounding as a threat to her taut nerves. The silence seemed to stretch alarmingly, and she said the first thing that came into her head.

'What time is it?'

A bark of derisory laughter greeted her comment. 'Don't worry, Helena, you still have a few hours' grace. I have reserved a suite of rooms at the hotel for our own personal use. I had thought we would have an hour or two to relax,' he taunted, 'before the reception, but fortunately for you we are late. The guests will already be arriving.'

It was with relief that Helen noticed the car was stopping. They had arrived at the hotel.

Carlo once again donned the mantle of devoted husband as he ushered her into the reception. He was magnificent, as an actor he would have outdone Olivier. From his impeccably tailored grey silk suit, to his hand-stitched shoes, he exuded an aura of dynamic masculinity without any effort. Helen could not help but be aware of the envious looks of most of the women present. A hollow laugh rose and died in her throat. God, if they did but know it, she would willingly have changed places with any one of them.

She grew increasingly tense as time rolled on, and it did not help at all to know Carlo was aware of it. He laughed and joked with all and sundry, apparently circulating but careful never to be far from her side. How was it, she wondered, that only she noted the mocking cynicism in his dark eyes as they flicked over her? Tonight he would take her, willing or not, and she wanted to scream at the thought of it. The past week he had assumed a mask of icy indifference that had given her a false sense of security, but now he was making no effort to disguise his intentions. Every time his gaze rested on her, his lips curved in a blatantly sensuous smile.

Helen drained the glass of champagne in her hand, and immediately reached for another one. She had drunk little all afternoon, and eaten even less, but now she felt desperately in need of some courage, even if it only came out of a bottle. Carlo's behaviour was inexplicable to her. She was sure he hated her. Over the past few days they had seldom spoken and, when they had, he had made no effort to hide his bitter enmity. She hadn't minded, it only served to bolster her confidence in the agreement they had reached. When she had thought of their wedding night, she had imagined a cold-blooded coupling, quickly achieved, with an equally quick pregnancy as the result. Now she was no longer so sure. By every look and touch, Carlo was doing his best to make her sensually aware of him, and worse, he was succeeding.

Thankfully she spied a passing waiter and, replacing her empty glass on his tray, took a full one, downing it in a couple of gulps. Carlo's arm encircled her waist, his fingers burning into her skin through the thin fabric of her dress as he tightened his grip, pulling her closer to his side. She could feel his muscular thigh, hard against her own, and could do nothing to control the tremor that coursed through her. Perhaps drinking was not such a good idea, after all, having the opposite effect than the one she desired. Instead of giving her courage, it must be lowering her resistance, she thought muzzily.

Then Carlo bent his dark head towards hers, and under cover of nuzzling her ear, stated in a harsh whisper, 'That's quite enough to drink, *mia sposa*. I have no intention of taking a drunk to my bed.'

Her fighting spirit was aroused. 'Tough! You'll just have to sleep on your own,' she bit back, trying to pull out of his grasp.

'Well, well! Dissent already, and the reception not over yet,' a familiar female voice interrupted, before Carlo could form a response to Helen's comment.

Helen groaned silently as she recognised the woman standing before them. The wide smile on the ruby lips was belied by the gleam of malice in the dark eyes, as they slid over Helen, to rest on Carlo with hungry intensity.

'Caterina, how good of you to come! Allow me to introduce you to my wife,' Carlo drawled, ignoring the woman's first remark.

'Oh, there's no need, Helen and I have met before. Didn't she tell you?' she cooed, one tiny hand curling over Carlo's free arm.

Carlo looked down at Helen, one brow arched enquiringly, and it was all she could do to mumble, 'Yes, we have met before.'

Caterina, in her sultry voice, continued, 'Allow me to congratulate you, Helen. Last week Stephano, and this week married to Carlo. You must tell me your secret,' she demanded suggestively.

Helen blushed at the implication, flashing a wary glance at her new husband, but he appeared to be amused by the bitchiness of the other woman, and laughingly responded, 'Ah, Caterina, you never change, always trying to make trouble. Stephano was looking after Helen for me...nothing more.'

He favoured the woman hanging on to his arm with a tender smile, to which she responded with a husky-voiced, 'You know me so well, *caro*. You must excuse my little joke, Helen, but Carlo understands. He and I are such very old...friends.' The last word was said with just enough hesitation so Helen could be in no doubt that it should have been lovers. 'But seriously, Helen, I wish you the very best, and I hope you will both be happy.'

Lying hound, Helen thought, while saying a polite thank you. Carlo was no help, content to stand listening to the exchange, a cynical smile on his handsome face. Helen could have taken the opportunity to move out of his hold, but didn't.

Carlo led her into the middle of the room, his arms folded firmly around her waist.

'What do you think you're doing?' Helen muttered, aware that everyone's eyes were upon them.

Carlo smiled down at her, saying softly, 'It is expected we start the dancing, so take that scowl off your face, or people may get the wrong impression.' He was tightening his hold on her as he spoke, the long length of him pressed firmly against her.

Maybe it was the champagne, or perhaps the challenge of the other woman, Helen did not know, but she no longer had any desire to resist the obvious invitation in Carlo's dark eyes. Relaxing against him, she rested her head on his shoulder, as they moved in perfect unison to the slow, romantic music of a love song.

The evening took on a dreamlike quality for Helen. Carlo stayed close to her side, and fielded some of the more ribald comments of his friends with a delightful humour that Helen found impossible to resist. Laughing up into his wickedly sparkling eyes at one such pithy comment, she was trapped and held by the dark intensity of emotion she saw there. Slowly, Carlo bent towards her and, brushing his lips gently across her mouth, whispered so only she could hear, 'I think it is time we left, Helena.'

Helen stood in front of the large ornate bed, paralysed, incapable of coherent thought. The sound of a door opening broke her trance and she swung round to see Carlo turning the key in the lock. Her heart raced as he walked towards her, shedding his jacket and tie as he did so. Stopping only inches in front of her, he slowly began unfastening his shirt. She watched, mesmerised, as he slid it off his broad shoulders and dropped it on the floor, her eyes following his hands as they went to the belt of his trousers.

'You don't intend to go to bed in that, do you?' Carlo asked softly, flicking one finger under the shoulderline of her dress.

'N-no. No,' she whispered as his hands caught her shoulders.

'Let me help you, *cara*.'

Helplessly she stood as he eased the soft tulle down over her shoulders to her waist and, lowering his head, gently licked just above the wisp of lace that outlined

NO COST! NO OBLIGATION! NO PURCHASE NECESSARY!

PLAY "LUCKY 7"
AND GET AS MANY AS SIX FREE GIFTS...

HOW TO PLAY:

1. With a coin, carefully scratch off the three silver boxes at the right. This makes you eligible to receive one or more free books, and possibly other gifts, depending on what is revealed beneath the scratch-off area.

2. You'll receive brand-new Harlequin Presents® novels, never before published. When you return this card, we'll send you the books and gifts you qualify for absolutely free!

3. And, a month later, we'll send you 8 additional novels to read and enjoy. If you decide to keep them, you'll pay only $1.99 per book, a savings of 26¢ per book. There is no extra charge for postage and handling. There are no hidden extras.

4. We'll also send you additional free gifts from time to time, as well as our newsletter.

5. You must be completely satisfied, or you may return a shipment of books and cancel at any time.

FREE—digital watch and matching pen

You'll love your new LCD quartz digital watch with its genuine leather strap. And the slim matching pen is perfect for writing that special person. Both are yours FREE as our gift of love.

PLAY "LUCKY 7"

Just scratch off the three silver boxes with a coin.
Then check below to see which gifts you get.

YES! I have scratched off the silver boxes. Please send me all the gifts for which I qualify. I understand I am under no obligation to purchase any books, as explained on the opposite page.

108 CIH CANM

NAME

ADDRESS   APT

CITY   STATE   ZIP

7 7 7	WORTH FOUR FREE BOOKS, FREE PEN AND WATCH SET AND FREE SURPRISE GIFT.
🍒 🍒 🍒	WORTH FOUR FREE BOOKS AND FREE PEN AND WATCH SET
● ● ●	WORTH FOUR FREE BOOKS
🔔 🔔 🍒	WORTH TWO FREE BOOKS

her firm breasts. Helen jumped as if she was scalded, but was incapable of pulling away.

She had agreed to this, she told herself, but it wasn't their agreement that kept her in his arms, rather an aching longing to feel the hard, muscled chest against her softer curves. Willingly, her lips parted as he covered her mouth with his own in a long, drugging kiss. She felt her dress fall to the floor as she ran her hands up through the soft hair of his chest to curve around his neck, prolonging the kiss. She knew it was wrong, but couldn't resist the dynamic pull of his masculinity.

Carlo swung her up into his arms, murmuring words she didn't register into the gentle curve of her throat. Laying her on the bed, he swiftly shrugged off the rest of his clothes and joined her. In the dim light of the room, the beauty of his naked form was a potent aphrodisiac to her bemused mind. He leant over her and she watched him in a kind of suspended animation as, one by one, he removed her underclothes, covering her now burning flesh with tiny kisses, as each flimsy garment fluttered to the floor. Then his mouth again found hers, their tongues meeting and probing, devouring each other. Carlo's hands on her breasts tormented them to a heavy fullness, her nipples rigid with longing.

His mouth closed over first one aching tip, then the other, until she was delirious with a sensuous excitement only he could arouse in her. Her hands gripped his shoulders in a spasmodic reaction, as her body arched up under him. He lowered his frame over her, allowing her to feel the full weight of him, murmuring husky words of love into her throat. The heavy pounding of his heart matched the racing beat of her own. Her eyes fluttered open as his hand slid between their two bodies to curve over the soft mound guarding the door to her femininity, his long fingers searching, stroking. She gazed up into his handsome face, flushed now with passion, his dark eyes gleaming black with a barely controlled desire.

'I want you, Helena, I want you... I can't wait.'

She couldn't speak, her throat was choked with emotion, but slowly she pulled his head down towards her, signifying her acceptance. Her long legs twined around his lean hips.

Quickly, he eased himself up slightly, groaning, 'God, I have waited six years for this.'

At his words, Helen froze, every muscle in her body clenching in instant rejection. How could he? her mind screamed. Six years ago he had been engaged to Maria. How could he remind her of his vengeance now?

'Oh, no. No! Don't do this to me,' Carlo rasped hoarsely, staring down into her huge green eyes.

Words of explanation rose in her throat but were never uttered, as his mouth ground down on hers, while his body drove deeper and deeper, at last drawing a response she couldn't hide. His huge frame shuddered uncontrollably, then he rolled off her to lie beside her, his erratic breathing the only indication of what had happened.

Helen turned over on to her side, her back to Carlo. She felt utterly degraded, used. The hurt was more intense than she had imagined possible. A masculine hand touched her shoulder and, in a soft voice, Carlo asked, 'Are you all right, *mia cara*?'

Pride made her shrug his hand off, and with bitter sarcasm she replied, 'I hope to God I'm not all right! I pray I am already pregnant, so I'll never have to suffer your touch again!' Leaping out of bed, she made straight for the bathroom, before he could stop her. She locked the door as the tears started streaming down her face, the shock of the last few days, along with a nagging emptiness in the pit of her stomach, combined to make her break down completely.

Eventually she stepped into the shower and, turning the water on full blast, she scrubbed every inch of her body, trying to eliminate his touch from her skin. Wrapped in a large fluffy towel, she rubbed herself dry, then tentatively she opened the door into the bedroom. The sound of Carlo's even breathing convinced her he must be asleep, and on tiptoe she walked across the room to the door. She cast a hasty look at the bed. The only illumination in the room was the moonlight gleaming through the window. Carlo was lying on his back, one arm spread across the pillow, the other hanging over the side of the bed, directly above where he had dropped his clothes. She quietly made her way to the opposite side of the bed, and carefully slipped beneath the cover. Carlo stirred once, but luckily did not awaken. Helen lay, staring into space, wondering if any other girl had ever had such a disastrous wedding night, until sleep overtook her.

She stirred, opening her eyes lazily, and for long moments wallowed in the warmth and comfort of the strong shoulder beneath her head, and the arm circled protectively around her waist. Then memory returned, and the events of the previous night flooded her mind. She sat up in shock as the realisation of whose arms she had slept in hit her.

Then, just as quickly, she slid back down the bed, as Carlo's sleepy voice drawled, 'Very nice,' reminding her she was naked. The towel she had wrapped around herself last night was lost in the bed somewhere.

She blushed scarlet, her heartbeat accelerating. 'I want to get up!' she yelped, pushing at the arm holding her.

'What's the hurry, Helena? Sophia and Tommaso are away for the weekend. We have only ourselves to please,' he husked, pulling her closer, his breath tickling her cheek as he spoke.

'Nothing you could possibly do would please me,' she gibed sarcastically, once again trying to remove his arm from her body. His fingers tightened on her waist as he raised himself on one elbow to look down at her flushed and angry face.

'Is that by way of a challenge, *mia sposa*?' he asked, grinning, his eyes gleaming with wicked amusement.

'As if I would dare challenge the great Signor Manzitti!' she derided, determined not to be seduced into compliance by the very masculine charm of the man, while admitting to herself that it was no easy task. Somehow this husband she did not want looked much younger and very appealing this morning, with his black hair tumbling in curls on his broad forehead, and a day's growth of beard darkening his chin. The grin vanished from his face as she watched.

'You're very brave this morning. Did last night teach you nothing?' he demanded coldly.

Still trying to remove his arm from her waist, but with no success, Helen cried, 'I can't bear you to touch me!'

To her surprise, Carlo made no comment, simply removing his arm from her waist. But before she could move he rolled over, trapping her beneath him. Still not speaking, he studied her intently, as though he had never seen her before, taking in the flushed, mutinous face, and long golden hair spread out in a tumbling mass across the pillow.

The effect of his naked body, touching her own from chest to toe, was having a disastrous effect on Helen's heart rate, and as his eyes slid lower, to her throat and beyond, she hated herself for the quickening of her pulse in her neck.

'So, I disgust you? You can't bear me to touch you?' he mocked cynically. 'Liar... You don't have to make me angry to get me to make love to you. Try asking me nicely,' he mocked, moving lower as he spoke.

The effect on Helen's senses was chaotic, as the tips of her breasts scraped against his broad chest. She stared at the darkly handsome face above her, and a shiver of apprehension sliced through her. Why was she baiting him? She was no match for him, and she knew it.

Turning her head to the side, she murmured in a much subdued voice, 'Please, can I get up now? There is no need for a post mortem on last night.'

'Coward,' he whispered softly, as his lips found the pulse beating madly in her throat, kissing, then gently trailing back up her neck to her lips. His tongue licked the corner of her mouth.

She trembled at his caress, but refused to turn her head, saying, 'Will you leave me alone?'

'No, I won't, *cara mia*. Last night, perhaps, I was a little rough, but you've got a lot to learn, if you imagined you could let me go as far as I had, then start to play games. But not to worry,' he drawled throatily. 'Now I will show you how it can be for us.'

It was well after midday, before Helen was alone in the bed. The last few hours had been a revelation and a torment she would not have imagined possible the day before.

Carlo had made love to her with a slow, sensual determination that had made a mockery of her attempt to lie rigid in his arms. Pinning her hands above her head with one of his, he had treated her body to a display of sexual expertise that, in minutes, had her writhing against his restraining hand. With lips, tongue and teeth he had explored every inch of her, his long fingers probing every secret part of her until she lay shuddering, every nerve-end on fire, her blood molten in her veins. Time and again he had driven her to the brink, only to hold back, until Helen, to her shame, had begged him to take her. His ultimate possession of her was a revelation, all resistance forgotten, as he plunged deep inside her. Her muscles tightened around him, urging him on, until the world exploded around her in a million pieces. Their bodies locked in a convulsive climax that neither could deny.

When he had finally left her, his parting words echoed in her brain. 'You are my wife, Helena. Mine, understand?'

She understood perfectly...

* * *

It was with relief that she watched him drive off to
Palermo on the Monday morning. Sophia and Tommaso
were back, all smiles and congratulations, and after a
few words to Sophia Helen made her way back upstairs
to the bedroom. She had dressed in a hurry earlier, the
reason for her haste bringing a blush to her cheeks.

She had awakened to the closing of a door, and in
that unguarded space between sleep and being fully
awake, she had watched, fascinated, as Carlo, completely unconscious of his nudity, had moved around the
bedroom collecting his clothes. The early morning sun
streaming through the window had outlined his in-
tensely male physique in a golden glow, his black hair
damp from the shower, a ruffled mass of curls.

'Sorry, I haven't time this morning, but hold that
thought till tonight, hmmm?' he said with mockery in
his tone.

Startled out of her surreptitious study of his muscular
body, she let her gaze fly to his face, the amusement in
his dark eyes telling her he had noticed her fascinated
appraisal of his naked form. In a flash, she had jumped
off the bed and shot into the bathroom, mortified, as
his laughter rang in her ears.

The last two days had not been quite as difficult as
she had expected... After he had left her in bed on the
Saturday, she had had a shower. Then, dressed in a
simple cotton frock, she made her way downstairs. It
took every ounce of pride she possessed to walk into the
kitchen, the sounds from within telling her Carlo was
there. Prepared for his mocking triumph, she was amazed
to see him standing over a pan on the stove, obviously
cooking something. As she entered the room, Carlo
glanced over his shoulder and asked, 'Mushroom
omelette and chips, OK? Sit down, they won't be a
minute.'

'Yes,' Helen replied, surprised. Pulling out a chair,
she sat down at the large pine table, her eyes lingering
on his broad back. He was clad in a short-sleeved knitted

shirt, and tight, washed-out jeans, with a tea-towel wrapped around his waist. She found it hard to believe he was the same man she had married only yesterday. She quickly lowered her eyes to the table as Carlo placed a plate in front of her and sat down facing her. Her eyes widened, her generous mouth lifting at the corners in the beginnings of a smile as she noticed the table's centrepiece. A large coffee mug, with an exquisite red rose in it.

Carlo, following her line of vision, said ruefully, 'The thought was there, but unfortunately the vase wasn't. I don't know where Sophia keeps a damn thing in this kitchen.'

Helen's smile turned into a soft chuckle and, lifting her head, their eyes met, genuine amusement sparking between them. Helen knew exactly what he meant; Sophia had made it plain the first day Helen had arrived that she did not like anyone in her kitchen.

'Come on, grub's up, don't let it get cold,' Carlo said, picking up his knife and fork and tucking in.

'Where did you learn a saying like that?' Helen asked between mouthfuls of fluffy egg. '"Grub's up" is hardly part of a standard English language course.'

'I was at the LSE for three years, and shared a flat in Earl's Court with two blokes from Manchester. I think I learnt more English from them than I ever did at the School of Economics,' Carlo opined, grinning broadly. 'Though not, perhaps, the Queen's English.'

'I didn't know you went to university in England,' Helen said, surprised. 'I went to the LSE myself, but only for the one year.' Then she stopped. What was she thinking of? A friendly relaxed Carlo was much more dangerous to her emotional stability than the cold man of the last week. And much harder to resist.

'Did you enjoy university life?' Carlo asked, apparently unaware of her abrupt stop. 'I know I did. We had some great times roaming around London. All-night parties where we drank foul wine and put the world to rights, unable to remember a word that was said, the next morning.'

Somehow, the image of Carlo as a drunken student, Helen found irresistible. 'Did you really? I can't imagine you ever being drunk,' she exclaimed laughingly.

'Oh, I was, I assure you. But what about you? I'm not that old. I'm sure university life can't have changed much.'

'I don't really know. I never mixed in the social side of things. Probably because I didn't stay in digs, but had to travel back and forth from home every day,' Helen found herself explaining.

'And I'll just bet that was your father's idea,' Carlo stated grimly, pushing his now empty plate to one side, and fixing Helen with a cynical look. 'No denial, *cara*?'

'I don't know what you mean,' she mumbled untruthfully. 'Could we go and see Mount Etna this afternoon?' she asked, in a blunt attempt to change the subject.

'Yes, why not? I always loved being your guide.' Accepting her abrupt change of subject without comment, and reaching across the table, he took her hand, turning it palm upwards in his own, his thumb lightly caressing the soft centre, adding sensuously, 'In everything.'

Her body flooded with warmth at his touch. She pulled her hand away and stood up, almost knocking her chair over in her haste.

Carlo laughed and, walking round the table, took her hand in his, saying. 'Come on, Helena. I have a new car. I only had it delivered last week, and I'm dying to give it a good run-in. You can have the honour of being the first passenger.'

The new car was a gleaming black monster, low-slung, with wheels that seemed far too big for it. It looked more like a lethal weapon than a motor car to Helen's untutored eyes.

The next hour passed in a blinding whirl of colour and speed. The few occasions when Carlo was forced to slow down provided vivid cameos of the countryside. When he eventually parked, in the middle of a field, of all places, she was too breathless to ask why, before he grabbed her hand and was leading her over the rough grass, to where a helicopter was waiting.

Tugging on his hand, she cried, 'Wait, Carlo! What is this for? Where are we going?'

Clasping her firmly around the waist, he swung her up into the open cockpit, saying, 'You wanted to see Mount Etna, so, your carriage awaits, my lady.' Leaping up to join her, he burst out laughing at the look of stunned amazement on her lovely face.

'But I thought we would walk!'

'No, it's too late in the day for that. But Nico here has kindly offered to give us a bird's-eye view.'

The view of the volcano from the air was too marvellous for words, not that they could talk, anyway, because of the noise. But Helen watched avidly as Carlo silently pointed out various craters. As they circled over the top, the red heat was clearly visible in the very depths, the sulphurous smell almost overpowering, and Helen was elated but delighted to return to the ground. After about half an hour in the heavy atmosphere, it was a relief to breathe the clear country air.

Back in the car again, Carlo said, 'I know a nice little restaurant along the road. We can stop for dinner.' Flashing her a sidelong glance, he added, 'Unless you would prefer to return home, and cook it for us.'

She watched him uneasily, biting her bottom lip with her teeth. Carlo's exuberant mood of this afternoon had made her forget the past, and for a while they had been the relaxed, easy companions of old, but now she wondered if his mocking cynicism had returned. Giving a slight shrug, she decided to take his question at face value, and answered accordingly, 'No, I think I would rather dine out,' adding truthfully, 'Anyway, I can't cook.'

Carlo flicked her a swift, indulgent smile, his hand resting lightly on her thigh for a second, flustering her more than she liked to admit.

'Don't worry, Helena, you can't be excellent at everything. The restaurant it is.'

They shared a huge lobster with a side salad, and Helen finished with strawberries and cream, while Carlo had cheese and biscuits. The whole lot was washed down with champagne, which the proprietor insisted on supplying free of charge, as he knew of their recent marriage and as Carlo was a valued customer from way back. The evening took on a party atmosphere when an old man started playing a piano accordion, and Helen had made no demur when Carlo took her into his arms to dance. Soon, everyone in the place had joined in, including the owner. Some time after midnight, Carlo suggested it was time they leave, but she was reluctant to go. Helen much preferred the spontaneous pleasure shown by the people in the restaurant at the news of their marriage, to the formal reception of the previous evening.

It was on the long drive home, alone with her husband, that the fear of the coming night filled her with nervous tension.

She went straight to bed, hoping that if she was asleep before Carlo came upstairs he would leave her alone. The hope wasn't realised, as he slid naked into the bed beside her not ten minutes later. Taking her in his arms, he made a mockery of her futile attempt to remain passive in his hold, as he skilfully aroused her to the heights of sensuous pleasure, until they lay, satiated, in each other's arms.

Sunday morning dawned bright and clear, another scorchingly hot day. Helen opened her eyes to see Carlo standing beside the bed, already fully dressed in casual white trousers and a fine shirt, holding a tray in his hands.

'Come on, sleepyhead, breakfast is ready.' Putting the tray down on the bedside table, he leant over her. Brushing her brow with his lips, he picked up the spare pillow. 'Sit up, *cara*.'

Helen was so surprised that she did. Blushing furiously, she grabbed the sheet and tucked it firmly under her arms, while Carlo plumped the pillow behind her, then handed her the tray.

'Sophia told me *focaccia* is still your favourite. I'm glad to see you haven't forsaken everything Italian in the last couple of years,' he opined, a self-satisfied smile on his handsome face.

The effect of his closeness, and the memory of how easily he had won her over last night, filled Helen with a burning resentment. 'I never stopped liking things Italian. It is only certain males I find hard to bear,' she retorted sarcastically.

'Sarcasm doesn't become you, Helena, and we both know you're lying. Don't we?' he demanded hardily, holding her rebellious gaze with a darkly knowing look. It was Helen who lowered her eyes first. 'Eat up, and get ready. I'm taking you out for the day.'

'I'm not sure I want to go out,' she muttered, smarting at his high-handedness. Picking up a piece of bread, she dipped it in the large bowl of coffee.

'Well, I don't mind, I can just as easily join you in bed, if your prefer,' he suggested mockingly.

'No! No, we will go out. I'll only be five minutes,' she spluttered, almost choking in the effort to get the words out over a mouthful of food.

She felt an utter fool as Carlo turned on his heel to leave, saying with amused cynicism. 'I rather thought you would change your mind. I'll meet you downstairs in ten minutes. No more...'

For some reason Helen could not fathom, Carlo had the ability to make her relax, even when she was determined otherwise. She asked him coldly where they were

going, and his smiling response broke down her barriers
with no effort.

'It's a mystery tour. Indulge me, hmm? It isn't every
week a man gets married.'

And she had . . .

CHAPTER EIGHT

THEY stopped at a dry dock in Palermo, and there Carlo showed her over the most marvellous forty-foot yacht. It was in the process of being refitted; modern in design, but all panelled mahogany and brass inside.

'I owe you a sailing weekend but, as you can see, it will have to wait a while,' Carlo explained. 'I thought we would spend the month of November cruising the Greek Islands.'

Helen turned a delighted face up to his. 'That would be great! I've never been to Greece before.' She completely forgot that this man was supposed to be her enemy. Later, after lunch in Palermo, he led her to the car. 'Today, I think we need a siesta,' he mocked as he slid behind the wheel, and in an amazingly short time they were back at the villa.

There was no doubt what he had in mind, and Helen was unable to mask the leaping response of her senses for more than a couple of minutes when he carried her upstairs to the bedroom.

Much later, over dinner, Carlo arranged that they would meet in town the next day at four. He wanted to arrange a bank account for her. She tried to object, but was quickly overruled, as he explained, quite reasonably, that as his wife she had a position to uphold in the community and, much as he approved of the clothes she wore, she would need a much more extensive wardrobe as his wife. When she pointed out that she did not expect to stay very long, he had cut her off with the comment, 'That remains to be seen.'

Helen was not disposed to argue. After a very rocky start, they seemed to have reached a degree of compatibility she would not have imagined possible a few days ago, and she had no wish to upset the rather guarded peace.

Helen had no doubt she would conceive a child quickly. Luckily, she was in the middle of her monthly cycle, the most promising time for conception, and her husband was a very virile man, as he had proved over and over again in the past two days. She was still clinging to her original idea that she would be able to return home within the year. The thought came unbidden to her mind that, the longer she shared Carlo's bed, the more dangerous it would be for her, for the likelihood of finding another man to share her life and make a home with would become more and more remote. Carlo was a vastly experienced lover who took her, against her will, to the heights of erotic sensuousness and beyond. Deep in her heart lurked the painful feeling that perhaps it was already too late. Later, when he suggested going to bed, her pathetic attempts at resistance were overcome by Carlo in barely a minute. Her only consolation was that, in the throes of passion, some tiny part of her remained inviolate...

Helen now slipped out of the mismatched shorts and shirt she had donned so hastily earlier and, opening the wardrobe door, searched for something cool and casual to wear. Sophia had moved all Helen's clothes to the master bedroom some time during the wedding day, probably at Carlo's instigation. Finally she settled on a blue Indian cotton dress and, pulling it on, decided to spend the rest of the morning exploring the villa. It was doing her no good at all, musing on her indomitable husband. She did not know enough about the male sex, nor did she have the experience to even begin to understand a complex character like Carlo, and she doubted if she ever would.

The villa was much larger than she had thought, and it was with a sense of adventure that she mounted the stairs that led from the first floor, in a curving arc, to the top floor. Double doors, set in the centre of one wall, opened into a huge room that ran the whole length of the house. It had obviously been designed as a family room, in direct contrast to the very formal rooms on the ground floor.

Helen looked out of the window, and her eyes focused on the smooth white semi-circle of beach, and the sea, gently eating at the gleaming grains of sand. She was reluctantly reminded of her grandmother's conversation on her wedding morning. It had not been very hard to push it to the back of her mind during the past three days, for she had scarcely had a minute on her own, but now she had no such excuse.

Thinking about it now, she could see that her grandmother's perception of her father was much more astute than her own. Helen had placed him on a pedestal—he was a hero and could do no wrong in her eyes—but, looking back down the years, she remembered certain situations and instances. Although they had seemed nothing at the time, now, with her new perception, she recognised he had been overtly protective. One afternoon, on a visit to Sicily years ago, she had accepted the invitation of a young student, who was helping out at the dig, to go for a drink at the local taverna with him. It had been perfectly harmless; they had sat outside, Helen drinking coffee while he had a beer, but her father had seen them and read the riot act, telling the young man she was far too young to be in a pub, completely ignoring the fact that they weren't. It had been after that, that her father had told her they were going home the next day.

The only other time her father had seen her with a boy had been when she was about seventeen. Timothy had been her doubles partner in the local tennis club and, the one time she had invited him to her home, her father had made it very obvious he did not approve; not by anything he said, but by adopting an aloof, icy politeness that left the young man in no doubt that he was unwelcome.

It had been her father who had insisted on a university education for Helen, and she had gone along with it. But when she had been offered a place in the halls of residence, again it had been her father who had insisted she travel the eighty-mile round trip every day, effectively excluding her from the social side of university life. Not that she had minded, because by then she had met Carlo.

With a shock, she recognised just how amazing that was. The holiday villa was on its own in the countryside, well away from Rome. The long weeks should have been spent in the garden or by the pool, with trips out at the weekend with her father, Maria and Andrea. Had the choice of holiday home also been to protect her? If it had, it had failed miserably because, the one time Maria had taken Helen to Rome, they had bumped into Carlo. No wonder Maria had told her not to mention meeting him to her father; as his wife, and the closest person to him, she must have known how he would react if he found out his darling daughter was actually meeting a man.

It was painful to have to admit that her grandmother was right. Yet, examining her own emotions, Helen realised she did not love her father any the less because she recognised he had been less than perfect. Instead, she could sympathise with him. Remembering the circumstances of his first marriage and her own birth, it was not surprising he had done everything in his power to protect her. She smiled grimly; he was wrong in one respect. Helen could never be promiscuous. The last two years had taught her that. Carlo was the only man who had ever aroused the sensual side of her nature, and she had a nasty feeling that, after the past few days, he was the only man who ever would.

Helen sighed with regret for what might have been, then gasped at the implication of where her thoughts were leading her. If she accepted that her father was not the impartial judge she had thought him to be, then she had to consider that her father's reasons for refusing to let Carlo marry her, need not have been the truth, or at least not the whole truth. Was it possible, dared she even consider, that Carlo's first proposal of marriage had been genuine?

Helen was so engrossed in her own tortured thoughts that it was a shock when Sophia walked in to ask if she would like lunch indoors or on the patio. She opted for the patio, thanking Sophia, and apologising for dragging her all the way upstairs. She had not realised it was almost one o'clock. After a meal of cold meat and salad, Helen made no demur when Sophia suggested that she take a siesta.

Driving into Palermo with Tommaso, Helen could not keep down a feeling of well-being. She had awakened from her siesta, refreshed and more alive than she had felt for over a week. Dressed in a cream silk skirt with matching camisole top, and high-heeled sandals, her mirror told her she was looking good, and she left the villa almost jauntily. But if anyone had dared to suggest that her high spirits might have something to do with the fact that she was going to meet her husband, she would have denied it vehemently, though perhaps not truthfully.

The countryside lazed, hot and parched in the afternoon sun, but with vivid splashes of colour brightening up the landscape, the deep, glistening turquoise of the sea never long out of view.

When they arrived in the city, Tommaso stopped the car outside a large, new-looking office block and, helping Helen from the car, led her into a huge glass-fronted foyer. Their arrival coincided with the swishing open of a door in the bank of lifts that covered one wall. Helen's eyes widened in surprise, as she recognised the occupants. Carlo, head bent, was talking softly to the woman at his side, his hand under her elbow as he guided her out of the lift. Caterina... Who else? Helen thought

grimly. The other woman looked like the cat who had
got the cream, and for some unknown reason Helen's
spirits plummeted. Her gaze rested on Carlo, who didn't
appear to have noticed them, or if he had, was in no
hurry to acknowledge their presence. It was Tommaso,
with a discreet cough, who finally attracted Carlo's attention, and even then he did not speak to Helen, but
thanked Tommaso and told him he could go.

Helen could feel the rage building up inside her at his
cavalier treatment, but before she could open her mouth
Caterina spoke, her big eyes gleaming maliciously.

'Why, how sweet, Helen! Coming to meet your
husband. What's the matter? Don't you trust him out
of your sight?'

Helen felt about two inches tall, and unthinkingly
blurted out the truth. 'He told me I had to...' Immediately she wished she could take the words back, as the
other two burst out laughing. Caterina, looking up at
Carlo knowingly, said, 'Well, Carlo, I can see you mean
to turn Helen into an obedient Sicilian wife.'

Carlo let go of Caterina's arm and, taking a couple
of steps, was in front of Helen. His hands grasped her
shoulders and, bending his head, he dropped a hard kiss
on her lips. She stood frozen in his hold, hardly hearing
his swiftly spoken, 'I married Helen for one reason only.
I wanted her for my wife, just as she is. So don't start
any of your machinations, Caterina, or else...'

Helen didn't register his denial, her mind was too full
of the implication of the other woman's words. How
could he...? How could he discuss her with his ex-
mistress, or mistress? But he must have done. Caterina
had used exactly the same words as Carlo when he had
insisted she marry him.

A pain sharp as a knife sliced through Helen. She had
thought Carlo all sorts of devil, but she had never imagined he would have stooped so low as to tell Caterina
the truth of their marriage. A vivid picture flashed
through her mind of her husband and this woman,

laughing over the 'poor little English girl', wed to
produce a child. Helen tried to convince herself she didn't
care what Carlo and Caterina thought of her, but it was
hard...

She did not know how they came to be outside, and
Caterina's, 'Don't forget, a week on Friday!' were the
only words that registered, as Carlo opened the door of
his car and hustled Helen inside.

Carlo half turned in the driving seat, his glance
lingering on the girl beside him. Helen, aware of his
scrutiny, stared directly ahead, taking deep breaths,
trying to control the rising tide of humiliation and anger
bubbling inside her, but Carlo's hand caught her chin,
forcing her to face him. Silently, she returned his stare,
unaware of the flickering of pain in the depths of her
green eyes.

'What's wrong, Helena?' he questioned gently. 'You
look rather pale. You did take a siesta? I told Sophia to
remind you.'

Such concern! she thought bitterly, her glance sliding
down to his lips, then hastily away. He sounded almost
as if he cared, but she knew how wrong that idea was.

'Yes, I did, thank you. And I feel fine,' she replied.
Carlo's hand still held her chin, and his thumb, softly
caressing her jaw, was doing her no good at all. In an
effort to get the subject away from herself, she asked
him sharply, 'Tell me, what did your friend mean about
a week on Friday?'

Letting go of Helen, he straightened in his seat and
started the car, a smile curving the corners of his lips.

'You should listen more carefully, *cara*, and you would
know. She invited us to a party.'

'Are you sure she meant me as well?' Helen couldn't
resist asking, sarcastically, then wished she hadn't, as
Carlo laughed.

'Why, I do believe you're jealous, Helena!'

'I am not,' she snapped. 'Why should I be? What you
and your mistress do is no concern of mine.'

'And who told you Caterina was my mistress?' he asked silkily.

The very softness of his tone should have told her to tread carefully, but she was too angry. Only a couple of days before coming here, it had been in the newspapers. Anyway, he wasn't bothering to deny it.

'It is common knowledge,' she retorted, 'and I read it in the newspaper,' she ended defiantly. Did he take her for a complete fool? She might be dumb, but not *that* dumb!

Carlo, taking his eyes from the road for a second, flashed her a hard, cynical look. 'And you believe everything you read in the newspaper, Helena?'

Her own innate honesty had her replying, 'Well, perhaps not everything, but in this case I have the evidence of my own eyes. I'm not blind, you know,' she bit out. 'That woman can hardly keep her hands off you!' A vivid impression of red-painted fingernails curling around Carlo's arm appeared in glorious technicolour in her mind's eye. She knew she was revealing more than she wanted to, but didn't seem able to stop.

'In some areas you are remarkably blind. You only see what you want to see, and you are jealous, *mia sposa*, though I know better than to expect you to admit it,' he said.

'Rubbish!' Helen declared, turning to look at him, thoroughly enraged by the amused mockery evident in his dark eyes. 'I can't understand why you didn't marry the woman. You're obviously well matched.' As she said it, she recognised it was true; Carlo and Caterina were two of a kind—polished sophisticates.

Restlessly, she raised her hands to her head; travelling in the open-topped convertible was playing havoc with her long blonde tresses. Anyone less sophisticated than herself would be hard to find, she thought wryly, trying to smooth down the tangled mass of hair, and wondering confusedly why she continued to try and bait

Carlo. What was she expecting from him? Whatever it was, it wasn't what she got.

She sat in stunned silence as he responded, quite seriously, 'Caterina is certainly a very experienced lady, but you forget she was married to my best friend for years. If she had wanted a family, she would have had two or three children by now. You, on the other hand, Helena, are young enough and healthy enough to produce a dozen children, with no trouble at all.'

Well, what had she expected? Carlo couldn't have put it more plainly if he had put it in writing exactly why he had married her. So why did she feel so disillusioned? It was obvious he would have preferred Caterina as his wife, but probably she could not have children. Helen had suspected it was more than revenge alone that had made Carlo insist on marrying her, and for a while this morning she had almost convinced herself that her father had been totally wrong, and that Carlo had some genuine feeling for her. What a fool she was! Her father's reasons might have been wrong, but his basic premise, that Carlo did not love her, had been perfectly correct.

Anna's explanation of Maria's and Carlo's engagement being purely for convenience, Helen accepted now. But it was glaringly obvious to her that, far from protecting Maria from any gossip by his frequent visits to the home of his friend, it must have been to protect Caterina... What better cover could Carlo have for carrying on an affair with his best friend's wife than to be engaged to the man's sister? As for marrying Helen, even that made sense. Carlo would never marry Caterina if she couldn't have children. The Manzitti dynasty demanded a son and heir, so what better way to resolve the problem than to marry Helen? Carlo admitted that his father was the one who wanted revenge for Maria's defection. By marrying Helen, Carlo had resolved his father's notion of the vendetta perfectly, with the added bonus of Carlo's own personal revenge for Helen having jilted him. His colossal ego wouldn't stand for being jilted, he had told her as much, and certainly not by a stupid young girl whom he had imagined he had eating out of his hand.

Helen's conclusion did nothing to still the spinning wheels of her mind. There was too much she didn't understand, and she hardly noticed that the car had stopped.

They completed their business at the bank in record time. Then Carlo took her to various shops, waiting patiently while she tried on numerous gowns, separates, suits—a whole new wardrobe, in fact—but Helen could raise little enthusiasm. The high spirits she had felt on leaving the villa earlier had faded into a dim memory. Sullenly, she went along with whatever her husband or the assistant suggested.

Carlo took her by the arm, and asked softly, 'What is the matter with you, Helena? I thought all women enjoyed buying clothes,' he opined, puzzlement evident in his tone. 'I wanted to please you,' he ended, smiling down at her. For a moment, she was fooled by his concern.

Then she told herself he was only being pleasant for appearances' sake, but even so she could not help responding cautiously, 'Yes, well, I think I have enough dresses.' She was not prepared to start an argument with him in the shop.

'Right, OK. We have one more call to make, then we'll go home.' Taking her arm, he led her outside, after telling the assistant to have everything sent to his home.

The last shop was an exclusive lingerie shop, and Carlo with an ease that told her louder than words that he was used to purchasing such garments, proceeded to pick a selection of exquisite silk and lace underclothes, négligés and more. She felt like kicking him, but contented herself with muttering every vile name imaginable under her breath, unaware that she was twisting a wisp of a bra in her hands.

'Not bras, I think, *cara*. You have no need of them,' he opined throatily. 'How about that, instead?' he asked, indicating a red teddy on a display model. His dark eyes lit with devilish amusement.

'I will never wear that!' she snapped. It was positively indecent, a wisp of red silk that laced up at the front, the sides virtually non-existent.

'Of course you will, Helena. Think what fun we will have when I unlace you!'

She went as red as the teddy at his suggestively voiced comment, while Carlo laughed out loud at her obvious embarrassment. The sound of his laughter was the last straw that finally snapped her slender control.

'When hell freezes over, buster...' she snarled, and marched out of the shop and into the car, seething with resentment. After five minutes, most of her anger had vanished and she began to regret her hasty action. By the time Carlo joined her it had disappeared completely, replaced by fear when she caught a glimpse of his darkly flushed face. He was furious.

Flinging a parcel in the back seat, he climbed into the driving seat. His fingers were gripping the wheel so tightly that his knuckles gleamed white with pressure. Helen cast him a sidelong glance; he was as tense as a jungle cat about to spring. She could see his chest heaving as he breathed deeply, fighting for control.

'I'm...' She began to apologise.

'Shut up! Shut up, don't say a word.' he bit out. Then, turning slightly, he fixed her with a look of such bleak contempt that she visibly cringed in her seat.

'Don't you ever, ever, do that to me again. You may not want to be my wife, but you are. And, if nothing else, I will have your respect,' he demanded with a slow, icy precision. Then, not waiting for her answer, he started the car.

They returned to the villa without another word being spoken. Sophia served dinner as soon as they returned, and the tense silence lasted throughout the meal.

Helen found herself wishing she had kept her mouth shut in the stupid shop. He had only been teasing, she knew, and after the past couple of days, when they had for most of the time shared the easy familiarity of old friends, he was entitled to think she would not object to his teasing. Now the icy barrier was back in full force. She told herself it was better this way, but deep down she regretted breaking their tentative new relationship.

Carlo left the dining-room, saying, 'I will have my coffee in the study. I have work to do,' adding a curt 'Goodnight,' as he walked out of the door.

Upstairs in their bedroom, Helen smiled wryly as she unwrapped the parcel lying on the bed, and found the red teddy, along with all the other lingerie. Selecting the least provocative of the nightgowns, she pushed the rest into a drawer and, stripping off her clothes, had a quick shower. Then she pulled the froth of white lace over her head and slid into bed.

If she needed any further confirmation of Carlo's involvement with Caterina, he gave it that night. She lay for what seemed like hours before she heard his footsteps along the hall. She tensed, whether in fear or anticipation, she was not sure, but she need not have worried. Without switching the light on, she heard Carlo go into the bathroom, then the shower running, and finally silence. The weight of his body depressed the mattress; her nerves clenched, anticipating the touch of his hand. She could feel the heat from his body so close to her; the clean male scent of him enveloped her, and it was some time before she realised he had turned his back on her and was sound asleep.

She was still trying to convince herself an hour later that the siesta she had taken that afternoon was the reason she was unable to sleep, and it had absolutely nothing to do with her husband.

Helen registered the faint ting of the receiver as she replaced it. It had been Carlo, explaining that he had not

time to return to the villa before attending Caterina's
party, and instructing her to have Tommaso drive her
into Palermo to meet him.

She sighed and sank down on the bed. She had
showered earlier and, dressed in a brief lace bra and
pants, had been about to apply her make-up, when Carlo
had called. The sound of his voice had a strangely un-
settling effect upon her, a feeling she appeared to be
experiencing more and more often lately.

Helen was rarely awake when he left their bed in the
morning and, if she was, after that first Monday's de-
bacle, she pretended otherwise. She knew little of how
he spent his time in Palermo, only seeing him in the
evening, over the dinner table. Sometimes not even then
and, on the nights he did not return till much later, he
never offered any explanation and she never asked. They
behaved as two strangers, their only meeting-point the
bed they shared. There was never again a repetition of
the Monday night. No matter how late Carlo arrived
home, whether she was asleep or not, he reached for
her...

Helen shuddered at the thought of her own helpless
surrender to him. Carlo's lovemaking never failed to
arouse her. Silently, with an almost clinical precision,
he drove her to the heights of ecstasy, until she lay exhausted in his arms.

She had spent the last two years convincing herself
that she hated him, but it was as nothing to the way she
now hated herself, night after night, in the aftermath of
passion—she dared not call it love—the weakness of her
own flesh filled her with humiliation. She could not bear
to look at him, sure she would see a familiar gleam of
triumphant mockery in his eyes.

The past fortnight had not been all bad. Carlo could
at times be an amusing and attentive companion, the
epitome of a new bridegroom, showering Helen with
tender loving care until she almost believed it was
genuine.

The previous Saturday they had lunched at his family home and, at his father's instigation, Carlo offered to show her around the estate. Mounted precariously on the back of a motorbike, her arms firmly around Carlo's waist, they had set off. To Helen's surprise, it was a very large estate. They drove past waving fields of grain, then careened through olive groves, finally stopping by a hillside, threaded with grape vines.

Carlo, his cold anger of the past week gone, explained how Sicily was the bread basket of Italy. Virtually anything grew in the fertile soil, and the estate was not only self-sufficient but very profitable.

Helen smiled to herself, recalling their walk between the long lanes of vines. She had picked a grape, and was just about to pop it in her mouth when Carlo knocked it out of her hand.

'I know I said they were for eating, *cara*, but you must wash them first.'

She gave him a mischievous smile and, planting one hand on her jutting hip, and the other behind her head, drawled, 'Peel me a grape, darling,' in her best Mae West imitation.

Carlo burst out laughing, and proceeded to do just that.

'I was only joking, Carlo, it doesn't matter,' she giggled.

'Not at all. Don't you know I would do anything for you? Now, open your mouth,' he demanded, holding a very mushy grape in his fingers. Obediently, she did as he asked, only to have his mouth cover hers. His tongue, delicately flicking, sent an arrow of fierce longing shuddering through her. When she could speak, she asked huskily, 'What happened to my grape?'

Pulling her into his arms so that they sank to the ground, Carlo murmured, 'I dropped it. I could not resist the temptation of your parted lips,' he vouched throatily, and once again covered her mouth with his, his whole length stretched out on top of her, pushing her into the soft earth. For long moments there was no sound except the heavy breathing of their hearts, then a voice broke into the silence.

'*Patrono*, are you all right?'

Carlo jerked as if he had been shot and, lifting himself on his elbows, turned his head.

'Yes. Yes, *Padre*, I'm fine.'

It was only then Helen realised someone was standing at Carlo's feet, and obviously had not noticed Helen. Her body was quite obliterated by Carlo's much larger frame. She could feel the laughter bubbling up inside her as a voice faded into the distance, saying, '*Scusi, scusi.*'

Looking up at Carlo, she was amazed to see he was actually blushing. His handsome face was positively beetroot.

'Oh, Carlo! I never thought I would see the day when you would blush,' she gurgled, as he stood up, pulling her to her feet.

'I don't know why you're laughing, Helena. You realise that was the priest, and he is a great friend of Rosa's. By the time we get back for dinner, not only will my father know I was tumbling with my wife among the vines, but probably everyone on the estate as well.'

'So, is that so terrible?' she queried, still laughing. Grinning sheepishly, he took her hand and led her back towards the motorbike, saying, 'No, you're right, it doesn't matter. It's just it hardly enhances my image as an international financier, hmmm?'

He had been right about the gossip. Over dinner it was obvious the old man knew what had happened, and was having great difficulty controlling his mirth, while Carlo cast dagger looks in his father's direction, daring him to laugh. After dinner, when his father softly suggested they should stay the night, to *save time*, Helen had thought Carlo would have a fit, so she hastily agreed before he could say a word.

Later, in Carlo's old bedroom, which had been left pretty much the same since he was a teenager, even to a pin-up of Sophia Loren on the wall, she had teased him about having a preference for brunettes. Later still, she made no resistance when he pulled her down on to the narrow bed. That night was the nearest she had ever come to losing all her will completely, as he made love to her with a slow aching tenderness she had never experienced before.

The mood continued over to the following day, when they went to Anna's and Aldo's for the afternoon. The children were determined to get Carlo in the swimming pool, but he adamantly refused. When Helen added her voice to the children's, he took her by the arm, and led her to one side. To her astonishment, he explained, *sotto voce* that there were some very tell-tale marks on his shoulders and back, and he did not want to embarrass her by stripping off in front of everyone. Helen had never thought of that, and was so touched by the genuine concern in his eyes, no trace of his usual mockery evident, she had involuntarily reached up and stroked her hands over his broad shoulders.

Carlo had smiled down at her, murmuring, 'You know, this is the first time you have caressed me, of your own free will, in two years.'

Her hands stilled on his shoulders, and their eyes locked. He was about to add something, when the mood was shattered by the arrival of Caterina. In the brief half-hour she stayed, Caterina managed to upset everyone except Carlo. She told the boys to be quiet, told Anna she was far too soft with the children and, while clinging to Carlo, she had smiled sweetly at Helen and told her she looked tired, adding that she knew just how tiring Carlo could be.

Helen told herself she should be thankful for Caterina's presence. At least the other woman's arrival had shaken her out of the bemused state she had been in all weekend, and reminded Helen forcibly of the circumstances of her marriage.

Sitting on the bed wasn't getting her ready to go out. Resolutely, Helen stood up and crossed to the dressing table. Eventually she would have to face the confusing emotions her powerful husband aroused in her, but not now, not when she had to spend the evening in the sexy Caterina's company. Even if Carlo was not having an affair with Caterina, there were still the words on her wedding night. He had waited six years, for revenge...

CHAPTER NINE

DETERMINEDLY, Helen surveyed her near-naked form in the mirror. Not bad, not bad at all… Her skin had taken on a deep golden tan, and the front of her hair was bleached almost white by the sun, giving a very pleasing effect. Sitting at the dressing-table, she brushed her long hair until it gleamed like a sheet of gold and, plaiting the sides, she twisted it into a small coronet on the top of her head, allowing the rest to hang loose down her back. Carefully, she applied her make-up, using more than usual, outlining her large eyes with a fine grey pencil, and thickening her lashes with a dark brown mascara. Her eyelids she shaded with a pale green shadow, deeper at the sides. Satisfied with the effect, she crossed to the wardrobe and selected one of the dresses Carlo had bought for her and slipped it on. It was a plain white crêpe sheath, sleeveless with a tiny mandarin collar, with a slit opening at the front that plunged down between her breasts. A slim matching belt fastened around the waist, and the skirt fell smooth and straight to the floor, but with a concealed slit, thigh high at the side. Sliding her feet into three-inch-heeled sandals, she took one last look in the mirror, spraying herself with her favourite perfume, *Miss Dior*, as she did so.

'Caterinas of the world, beware,' she muttered to herself as, turning on her heel, she made her way downstairs.

Tommaso wasn't in the least put out at having to drive her into Palermo at such short notice, and when they arrived at the office block he insisted on accompanying her up to her husband's office. The lift stopped at the twelfth floor, and Helen followed Tommaso out, across a wide hall to a single door that she assumed was the entrance to Carlo's office; only it was not an office, but a penthouse apartment.

Carlo opened the door himself. He was wearing a dark brown towelling robe that reached to mid-thigh, and obviously nothing underneath. Smoothly he dismissed Tommaso and, taking Helen's arm, led her through a small hall into the lounge, saying, 'Help yourself to a drink, *cara*, while I finish dressing.' Turning, he disappeared through a door at the side. Helen was left with her mouth hanging open, looking around her in bewilderment.

It was a comfortable room, decorated in warm browns and tweeds: very masculine, very Carlo. It had never entered her head that he had a flat in town. Walking across to the huge window, she stood gazing out at the balcony, but seeing nothing. How stupid she'd been! No wonder he was often late home, he probably entertained his friends here. Her insides curled into a tight knot of disappointment. There was no sense in deluding herself, she didn't like the idea, not a bit. Perhaps she was wrong, perhaps it wasn't *his* apartment. The sound of a door opening had her spinning around to see Carlo, immaculate in a white dinner-jacket, walking towards her.

'Is this your apartment?' she asked, her eyes skidding over his tall frame, and back to his face.

'Of course. The whole block belongs to me,' he responded, grinning widely. 'Why? Whose did you think it was, Caterina's?'

Resentment rose, like bile in her throat, that he could mock her so openly. 'You never told me you had a flat in town,' she accused sharply.

'You never asked me.' His dark eyes narrowed in speculation on her hot face. 'So far in our marriage, you've shown no interest in where I go or what I do. Why the sudden curiosity?'

She had no explanation, at least, none she wanted to give him. Unable to withstand his scrutiny, she turned back to the window, mumbling, 'I just never realised you had a flat.'

'I have three, *cara*. Another in Rome and one in Buenos Aires.' It had not been a good idea, turning her back on him, for his arms slid around her as he spoke, one hand curving under her breast and the other across her stomach.

'Would you like a list of my assets?' he asked softly, his warm breath caressing her ear.

'That isn't necessary,' she got out, his closeness setting off alarm bells in her brain.

She could feel the heat of his body enveloping her, and blushed scarlet, as he husked, 'You already know my biggest asset.'

'No!' she squeaked, as the hand on her ribcage, slid up to cup her breast, and his other hand rubbed softly over her belly.

'Of course you do, *mia sposa. You* are,' he chuckled, and Helen was unprepared for the flush of pleasure his words aroused in her. It was with only the greatest effort that she prevented herself from sinking back against him. She was glad she hadn't when he continued, reminding her why they were married.

'Have you thought, Helena, that my child could already be growing inside you?'

Ignoring his provocative comment, she pulled out of his hold, not willing to admit how much it hurt to be viewed as some kind of breeding machine.

'It is time we were going,' was the most she could offer, as she walked quickly to the door.

Caterina's house was beautiful. Approached by a long steep drive, it was perched on the top of a hill, over-looking the marina, a blaze of light in the night sky. Carlo, taking her arm, led her into a huge lounge, over-flowing with people. To Helen's bewildered eyes, half the population of Palermo seemed to be present. Massive patio doors opened on to the terrace and gardens, and coloured lights twinkled in the trees around the patio, where tables and chairs were placed in a circle, leaving a small clear area in the middle for dancing.

They had hardly walked into the room before their hostess appeared, looking sexy as hell in a slip of red that passed as a dress. In seconds, Caterina had grabbed Carlo's arm, and was leading him towards a corner of the room where the bar was set up, while Helen trailed along behind, feeling like a spare part. It was going to be that kind of night, she just knew it.

At the bar, the other woman turned her big brown eyes on Helen and said, oh so sweetly, 'Do you know, Helen, I can't think how we didn't meet long ago. Carlo only told me a few days ago who you are. Why, we are related by marriage! Isn't it amazing?'

Helen didn't think it was amazing at all, and she knew perfectly well the only reason Caterina had said what she had was to let Helen know she had been meeting her husband. After finding out about the apartment earlier in the evening, it did not come as any great surprise, but the thought of the two of them using it sent a shaft of pain like a knife through her heart.

Perhaps that was why she answered bitchily, 'Yes, it is. I should call you *Aunty* Caterina, really.'

The older woman did not like that at all and, handing Carlo a drink, she turned spiteful eyes on Helen, saying, 'That's not necessary, dear. Caterina will do.' Then she added, 'Help yourself to a drink, Helen.' Pointedly glancing at the glass in Carlo's hand, she continued, 'Carlo's tastes I already know so well.'

Helen could not help the smile that curved her lips. The woman was so obvious it was laughable, but she wasn't going to let them have it all their own way.

'Why, thank you, Caterina. I'm sure you do.' Raising her eyes to her husband, she tacked on bitingly, 'You and a couple of hundred others, no doubt.' She watched the quick flare of anger in Carlo's eyes, but before he could say anything, she flashed him a brilliant false smile, and added, 'I'm sure you two will excuse me. I need some fresh air.' Carlo, with a glass in one hand and Caterina on his other arm, could do nothing to stop her and, turning quickly, she left them.

That's telling them, she thought mutinously, making her way out on to the terrace. Let him play around with his lady friend; *she* was going to enjoy herself. She was fed up with going in fear of the man, and anyway there was nothing more he could do to her that he hadn't already done. There was another bar outside. Quickly she crossed to it, giving the young man who was serving, a brilliant smile. She asked for, and got, a large gin and tonic. After emptying the glass in record time, she felt great and, seeing her husband was still indoors, deep in conversation with Caterina, she shrugged and ordered another drink. With surprise, she recognised the man with them as Diego Fratelli. They obviously did not need her company...

The younger element of the party were really getting into the swing of things. The disco beat sounded loud and clear on the night air, and Helen longed to get up and dance, so when a hand touched her elbow she turned, a willing smile on her face, to find Stephano eyeing her warily.

'Am I forgiven, Aunty?' he asked cheekily.

Helen had to laugh. 'Aunty, indeed! You could have warned me, Stephano.'

'If I had, I would never have got you on the plane,' he answered, grinning. Then on a more serious note, 'I did it for the best of reasons, Helen.'

She looked at his boyishly handsome face, and couldn't find it in her heart to be angry with him. The couple of times they had met since arriving in Sicily, Helen had had no chance to tackle him about his deceit in bringing her to the island, and somehow it didn't seem to matter any more. It was too late...

'What do you mean, the best of reasons?' she questioned hardily. 'Best for whom?'

'Why, me, of course!' he responded, laughing. 'Carlo would have killed me if I hadn't. Am I forgiven?'

Helen had to smile. Stephano was incapable of being serious about anything, and she could understand his feelings. Didn't she have the same trouble trying to say no to Carlo? 'Yes, I forgive you.'

'Great, I knew you would, and if you don't mind me saying so, you look marvellous. Married life must agree with you,' he opined, blatantly ogling her slender figure.

Helen shook her head and, smiling wryly, linked her arm in Stephano's, allowing him to lead her on to the dance-floor.

She had spent far too much time lately chewing over the past, when basically she was a realist. At the end of her relationship with Carlo years ago, she had determinedly put him out of her mind, and continued with her life. It had been hard, but she had succeeded eventually. Then, on the death of her father and Maria, another traumatic experience, she had done what she had to, giving up her university career for the less expensive alternative of the secretarial course, and again she had succeeded. Her marriage was a fact and could not be changed, and if her husband preferred another woman's company, so be it. She owed it to her own sense of self-respect to make the best of her circumstances. So, recklessly, she flung herself into the pulsating beat of the disco music with wild abandon.

The crowd of people Stephano knew were about Helen's age, and all good fun. In no time at all, she found she was thoroughly enjoying herself. She was a good dancer and a constant stream of dark-eyed young men fell over themselves to partner her, as well as keeping her constantly supplied with drinks.

When Stephano finally claimed her again, he quipped, 'Miss Cool, indeed! If the folks from the office could see you now,' he mocked, grinning at her flushed face, and gleaming mass of dishevelled hair. 'You're some mover, Aunty.'

'You're rather neat yourself, nephew,' she rejoined, giving him one of the blatantly sensuous looks he was so fond of casting over every woman he saw; but she could not keep the amusement from her eyes, and they both burst out laughing.

Eventually the mood of the party changed, the loud beat of the music replaced by slow, romantic numbers, and Helen sank gratefully on to a seat, while Stephano went to get them a drink.

She had not seen Carlo for some time. No doubt he was enjoying himself with his more sophisticated friends, she decided. She lifted her hand to her nape, running her fingers through her long hair; all the dancing had made her hot.

'All alone, Helen?' She looked up, to see Diego Fratelli standing beside her.

'Hello, Diego. I thought I saw you earlier. I didn't know you lived here.' Helen liked the man. He had been kind to her when they had met, so she smiled broadly up at him.

'I don't. I'm on holiday for a while. I've been watching you dancing, but only now has the music got around to my tempo. Would you do me the honour?'

'Yes, certainly,' she responded, casting a quick look around as she stood up. There was no sign of Stephano with the drinks. 'I would be delighted.'

He was a good dancer, not holding her too tight, and it was comforting to glide slowly around the dance-floor. Diego was the perfect partner, making easy small talk, so she relaxed completely in his arms, only tensing when he mentioned Carlo.

'You really surprised me, Helen. I had not realised you were engaged to Carlo when we first met, though I should have guessed. It was obvious Stephano wasn't the man in your life.' His friendly eyes smiled into hers. 'Carlo is a very lucky man.'

Before Helen could reply, a strong hand grasped her shoulder and the voice of her husband sounded loud behind her, 'I know I am, Fratelli, and I intend to stay lucky. So, if you will excuse us?' Almost dragging Helen out of the other man's arms, he clipped, 'Our hostess is looking for you.'

Helen gave Diego an apologetic glance as Carlo's arm curved around her waist. His returned look was sympathetic as he murmured, 'So that's it. Till next time, Helen.' Turning on his heel, he left.

Helen was so mad that she could hardly speak. How dared he stroll up and grab her like that? Green eyes spitting fury, she let fly with, 'My God, you've got some nerve! You could at least have been polite to the man.' Possibly all the drinks she had consumed made her reckless, for she ignored the dark anger in his eyes, and continued, 'You spend all evening with your friends, then have the cheek to look affronted because I danced with Diego.'

Carlo's arms closed around her, and his fingers slid tantalisingly up her back. Holding her close, swaying to the music, he said, 'Is that what you call it—dancing? The man was almost making love to you!' he opined bluntly.

'Don't be ridiculous!' she snapped back.

'It is your behaviour that is ridiculous, *cara*, not mine. I have watched the exhibition you have given all evening, and I won't stand for it. You are my wife, remember?' he stated emphatically, one long leg nudging between her thighs, guiding them clear of the other dancers.

'Your wife? My exhibition?' she exclaimed. 'What about you, flaunting your mistress in front of everyone?' How dared he criticise her behaviour? 'Why, if it hadn't been for Stephano and his friends, I would have spent the whole evening sitting on my own,' she declared bitterly, stumbling over her own feet in her agitation.

Carlo steadied her, one hand tightening on her waist, his other stroking her neck. His fingers twined in her hair and, he gently tugged her head back, so that her angry green gaze locked on his dark unfathomable eyes.

Helen felt the anger drain out of her, suddenly aware of his muscular hardness so close to her. She raised her hands to his chest to push him away, but found instead her heartbeat quickening. The feel of his warm flesh through the silk of his shirt was so pleasurable that her fingers tingled at the contact.

She lowered her head, incapable of sustaining his scrutiny, as he admitted, 'You are right, Helena, and I apologise. Perhaps I did neglect you earlier—my only excuse is that it was business.'

Business, my eye! she thought dully, then was thrown into utter confusion by Carlo's next statement.

'There has been so much distrust and misunderstanding between you and me, perhaps this will help. But listen well, for I am only going to say it once. Caterina is not, nor has she ever been my mistress.'

Helen's head jerked up at his words; carefully she studied his handsome face, looking for some sign, some indication, that what he was saying was the truth. His behaviour was so unusual, never had she known him apologise for anything; and to declare Caterina was nothing to him was so out of character. He was not the sort of man to justify his actions to anyone, and certainly not to Helen.

'You didn't have to tell me that,' she remarked warily, puzzled by the tender gleam in his brown eyes.

'No, I know, *cara*, but I'm tired of fighting with you.' Pushing her head down on to his shoulder, he cradled her in his arms, voicing huskily, 'Let's spend the rest of the night as friends. After all, it is our wedding anniversary.'

'Wedding anniversary?' Helen questioned hazily, lost in the sensuous warmth of Carlo's embrace.

'Mmm, two weeks today,' he murmured, his words lost as his warm breath invaded her mouth, and her lips parted willingly beneath his. Helen surrendered completely, her body melting against his harder frame. Why

fight it? she told herself, this was where she had wanted
to be all night.

The rest of the evening was like a moment out of time.
The star-studded sky, the twinkling lights and soft music
all conspired to enhance the magic of the hour. Helen
slid her hands under his jacket to caress his broad back.
Clasped tight in each other's arms, not a centimetre between them, they swayed sensuously to the soft beat of
the music.

Later, hand in hand, they made their way back indoors, and Carlo, leaving her for a moment, came back
with two plates loaded with food: tiny vol-au-vents
stuffed with prawns, slices of pizza, salad and a selection of cold food. After eating, they drank coffee and,
to Helen's delight, when Caterina appeared, asking Carlo
to dance, he dismissed her quite curtly.

It was after three in the morning when they returned
home. Helen, leaving Carlo to garage the car and secure
the house, went straight upstairs to their bedroom.

It had been a strange evening, much more enjoyable
than she had first envisaged. Slipping out of her dress
and kicking off her shoes, she made for the bathroom,
her hands busily undoing the coronet of hair on top of
her head. With a brisk shake, she set it free to tumble
around her shoulders. Stretching lazily, she unclipped
her bra, then carefully removed her eye make-up.

She was still feeling slightly bemused by Carlo's odd
behaviour. He had never before shown any desire for
her company, except in bed...so why, tonight, did he
suggest they be friends? She had racked her brains on
the long drive home, but could come up with no ap-
parent reason.

'Do you intend to spend the rest of the night in the
bathroom, Helena?'

Startled, she swung round. Carlo was leaning negligently against the doorframe, naked, except for tiny
black briefs that did nothing to hide his obvious masculinity. Her eyes skimmed restlessly over him. He had

a beautiful body, muscular and long-limbed, the fine
covering of black hair on his chest arrowing enticingly
downwards. Helen gulped at her errant thoughts, her
pulse-rate rising alarmingly. The hazy, romantic mood
of earlier was replaced by an electric tension.

Shaken, she tried to hide her instant response to him
by crossing her arms over her breasts. 'I was just coming,'
she answered resentfully, asking herself, and not for the
first time, why this man had such an alarming effect on
her. She should hate him but, as he straightened and
walked towards her, it wasn't hate she was feeling, but
an overwhelming urge to reach out and touch him.

He stopped about a foot away from her and, clasping
her wrists, he gently unfolded her arms from her breasts.
Holding them pinned to her sides, he said, 'Why so shy,
Helena? I *am* your husband,' he grinned, then added
throatily, 'I won't bite, not unless I think you want me
to, *cara*.'

He allowed his gaze to drop to the pink-tipped
mounds, taut and inviting. She heard his quick intake
of breath and colour flooded her face. Ashamed of her
own arousal, she wished the ground would open and
swallow her up.

His dark eyes lifted to hers, glittering dangerously, then
softened as he registered her embarrassment. 'It never
ceases to amaze me that you can still blush.'

Helen was incapable of speech, as the nerves in her
stomach knotted at the look in his eyes. Carlo shook his
head and, laughing down into her lovely face, he grasped
her hand firmly in his own, while his other hand flicked
lightly across her breasts.

With a sigh, he growled, 'Come on, I have something
for you,' as he led her into the bedroom.

Submissively, she allowed him to lead her. He let go
of her hand, and she stood rooted to the spot. She felt
like an idiot; this near-naked, laughing, teasing Carlo
had thrown her completely off balance. Her thoughts
and emotions were chaotic and when, taking her hand,

Carlo placed a long leather box in it, her confusion was complete.

Warily she opened it, and there on a bed of white velvet was the emerald necklace she had tried on at Aldo's. It was magnificent! Emotion choked her as Carlo took the necklace from its resting place and, carefully brushing her hair out of the way, fastened it around her throat.

Their eyes met in the mirror: hers questioning, his guarded, almost hesitant.

Helen raised one slender hand, her fingers tentatively touching the jewels, sparklingly reflected in the mirror, the picture they made against her naked flesh wildly erotic. A single table lamp was the room's only illumination, and Carlo appeared as a huge dark shadow looming over her, strangely protective.

When his hands closed over her shoulders, a melting warmth surged through her and, sighing, she leant back into him.

'Why, Carlo?' She could not begin to understand his reason for such a gift.

'I bought it for your wedding present, but, well, our wedding night didn't turn out quite as I intended,' he mocked, a tinge of self-disgust evident in his tone. Then, softly, he explained, 'I wanted it to be perfect for you, and in my arrogance, I thought my wanting it so would make it so. When you froze up on me, I was bitterly angry. Pride, I suppose.'

The import of his comment shocked Helen rigid. He had wanted it to be perfect for her? But that would mean he really cared! Turning her head, no longer content with his reflected image, she studied his darkly handsome face but, evading the enquiring look in her luminous green eyes, his strong hands moving restlessly on her shoulders, he continued, 'Well, anyway, Helena, do you like it?' he questioned, almost as though he was afraid she would refuse his gift.

For an instant she was going to do just that, but some deep feminine intuition stopped her. Her glance fixed

on the jagged scar on his temple; she was responsible
for hurting him once before, and the guilt still lingered.
She could never do anything to harm him, she knew that
with certainty. Why, she did not want to examine, but
she recognised that refusing his gift would hurt him. Tonight, for a while, he had shown her what their marriage
could be like, if she let it, and it seemed to Helen, as
his hands left her shoulders to wrap around her waist,
enveloping her with his warmth, that the question he
was asking was bigger than the one he had voiced.

She could feel the tension in him as he waited for her
answer. Turning fully in his hold to face him, her hands
resting lightly on his chest, she gave him her answer.

'I love it, Carlo. It's the most beautiful thing I've ever
seen.' Raising herself on tiptoes, her hands gripping his
broad shoulders, she brushed her lips along his firm jaw.
'Thank you,' she breathed. 'But I'm ashamed to say, I
never thought to get you anything.'

His response was immediate, his harsh face trans-
formed by a wide smile of pure joy. His brown eyes
gleamed with a latent sensuousness, as his arms tightened
around her.

'Oh, Helena, don't you know?' he mocked briefly.
'The only thing I have ever wanted is in your power to
give.'

She did not fully understand his words, but at four
in the morning, tired, and suddenly tremblingly aware
of their nakedness, she was in no condition to think.
When his head lowered to hers, she gave up trying.

His lips teased tiny kisses over her eyelids, the soft
curve of her cheek and along her jawline. Finally, his
mouth closed over her parted lips in a kiss of such aching
tenderness, she thought her heart would burst. All her
senses were trained on the firm male body, so close...
Her breasts hardened against the muscular wall of his
chest, the surging heat in his loins evoking a reciprocal
heat in the pit of her stomach.

She barely registered his groaning plea. 'Please, Helena, give yourself to me. Don't fight it. Touch me as I know you can,' he begged, one hand lacing through her hair while his tongue flicked around the contours of her mouth. 'Don't make me take you, *cara*.'

Carlo's rasping words, his mouth against her throat, the dampness of his flesh against her, finally broke down her self-imposed restraint of the last couple of weeks. She no longer had the ability or the desire to fight him, and her slender hands roamed at will over the sinewy muscles of his back, and up into the silky blackness of his hair. She felt a wild delight at the long shudder that racked his frame at her tacit acceptance of his plea.

'I want you,' Carlo groaned, his voice hoarse as he swiftly picked her up and carried her to the bed, collapsing on to it. 'God, how I want you!' he mouthed.

In seconds, he removed the last remnants of their clothing. His lips trailed a path of fire down her throat. Thousands of pounds of jewels were cast on the floor, like so much litter, for he found them an impediment to his goal—the pulse that beat madly in her neck.

Trembling, Helen stroked the curve of his thigh, her hands shaping his narrow waist. Her last restraint gone, she gloried in the feel of his satin skin. Then Carlo lifted her over him, taking the hard tip of her breast into his mouth. Helplessly she arched back, her legs tangling against his thighs. A low moan, from the very depths of her throat escaped as his name. 'Carlo! Oh, Carlo.'

'Say it, Helena. Tell me you want me.' He looked up at her with demanding eyes.

'I want you, I want you,' she gasped, collapsing against him, her mouth, finding his hard male nipples, licking, biting. Her legs parted over his thighs. Hotly, she writhed over the hard male core of him, a teasing torment she burnt for. Her mouth found his and her tongue probed, demanding his full possession. Her green eyes glazed with passion, she raised herself slightly to look down into his darkly flushed face. 'Now, Carlo, now!' she groaned her need.

His gaze locked with hers, his hands curving around her hips, lifting her slightly. Then, gently, he probed the hot silky centre of her, his hands sliding up to caress her hard breasts.

She closed her eyes, throwing her head back, her hands on his chest. She could not wait for his tentative approach, she was burning up, her nerve-ends stretched to breaking. Fiercely she pushed against him, taking the whole of him inside her.

As if it had been a signal Carlo was waiting for, he spun her over beneath him, surging into her with such force that Helen gasped. Her hands curved over his firm buttocks, urging him on, until together they reached a shattering crescendo.

Carlo rolled on to his side, their bodies still joined. 'So now we know, Helena, that you ache with the same gut-wrenching pain I do... You would never admit it before, but after what we have just shared, *cara*, you will never again be able to deny it,' he murmured softly, his hand gently stroking her hair from her face. He smiled teasingly.

Helen knew he was right, and for once she did not care that she had betrayed her feelings for him. Snuggling into his warmth, she could feel him moving again inside her, and with a secret, sensuous smile on her lips, she looked innocently up at him, saying submissively, 'Yes, Carlo.' She moved her hips suggestively against him as she spoke.

Carlo laughed softly, his black eyes gleaming with pure masculine triumph, and a wicked intent. 'Ah, Helena, I have my emerald-eyed little wanton back! God, when you are like this I could make love to you all night.'

And he did...

To Helen, their lovemaking took on a dreamlike quality. They exchanged long, drugging kisses, mouth on mouth, limbs entangled, her silk-skinned body melded to his satin-sheathed frame. Sweat-slicked and moist with love, they were surrounded with the scent of love.

Carlo's long fingers stroked and probed her thighs, stomach, her breasts, every erogenous part of her, while her slender hands explored his every muscle and sinew, playfully teasing, tugging on his soft body hair. Until, finally, hearts pounding in unison, they rode the sea of love on crashing waves of passion. Submerged, as one they plunged to the uncharted depths, that void of blackness where for an instant life ceases, only to be tossed back to the surface of consciousness in a cataclysmic surge of pure energy, to lie shuddering in each other's arms, exhausted, spent.

Carlo's raspingly voiced, 'We have to talk, *cara,*' was only faintly heard by Helen, as sleep claimed her.

The faint sound of voices drifted in through the open window. Helen stretched lazily, like a contented cat, in the huge bed. As she turned on her side, her eyes fluttered open as she reached out a hand... Then, instantly, she was wide awake, the memory of the previous evening filling her mind.

She was alone. The only sign of her husband's earlier presence was a deep indentation on the opposite pillow. In an agony of self-recrimination, she relived their lovemaking of the night before, her body burning at the memory. What had he said? 'He had his emerald-eyed little wanton back.' How true, she thought bitterly, forced at last to accept her own deeply sensuous nature. She groaned; the self-knowledge gave her no happiness. For weeks, she had convinced herself she could marry Carlo and walk away unscathed, after fulfilling her part of their bargain. What a fool she'd been! Last night she had wanted him, gloried in his possession, and worse. In a flash of blinding clarity, she knew she loved him, and always had done, since the day they had first met.

For two long years she had fiercely denied her emotions, but last night her capitulation had been com-

plete. There would never be another man for her, only
Carlo. To have his child, then walk away, would break
her heart into a million pieces. How could she have made
such an agreement? With a despairing sigh, she buried
her head in the pillow, the slight, lingering scent of Carlo
stirring her distraught emotions.

He must never realise how great a victory he had won,
she vowed silently. They had made a bargain, and she
would have to stick to it. His expressed intention to turn
her into an 'obedient Sicilian wife' rang in her brain.
How he would gloat if he found out how successful he
had been! The way she felt about him, she would be
overjoyed to be allowed to stay with him, but she knew
her pride would not let her admit as much.

Sophia, entering with a coffee tray, informed her it
was one in the afternoon. Wryly, she told herself that
last night had had one good effect, at least: she had obviously slept well.

Washing and dressing quickly, in lemon shorts and a
matching halter top, Helen made her way downstairs.
She was wary of seeing Carlo, but it was no good putting
it off, and the voices she'd heard indicated that he was
not on his own. That must surely be to her advantage.
He could not pass any gloating remarks with someone
else present.

The visitor turned out to be Stephano, who took one
look at Helen as she walked out into the sunlight on the
patio in her brief shorts and top, and said, grinning
cheekily, 'Good morning, Helen. Or should it be good
afternoon?' he laughed, adding, with a knowing glance
at Carlo, 'Is this sexy uncle of mine wearing you out?'

Helen blushed furiously, her eyes flying to Carlo, who
leant negligently against the terrace wall. Dressed in old
denim cut-offs and nothing else, he looked years
younger, and incredibly attractive. He was obviously not
in the least offended by Stephano's comment as, catching
Helen's eyes, he smiled.

She was stunned by the warmth in the depths of his brown eyes. Her heartbeat raced as he moved towards her, throwing a casual arm around her shoulder, and laughingly telling Stephano, 'You should not tease my wife. She is not used to your outspoken ways yet.' Bending forward, he placed a gentle kiss on her half-open mouth.

She couldn't think what had come over her arrogant husband but, whatever it was, she was grateful. Daringly, she slid her arm around his waist, the feel of his smooth skin beneath her fingers intoxicating.

'Are you all right, Helena?' he asked softly.

Hesitantly, she smiled up at him. 'I'm fine,' she breathed. 'I'm sorry I overslept. You should have sent Sophia earlier.'

'No, *cara*, you deserved your beauty sleep,' he husked, ignoring Stephano. Turning her fully to face him, he opined throatily, 'Last night was marvellous.' His hands gently squeezed her shoulders, and he succeeded in confusing Helen completely.

Where had the cold, bitter man of the last few weeks gone? she wondered, searching his expression for some sign of his usual mockery, but finding none.

'Hey, I hate to break it up, you two, but Carlo only has an hour to catch his plane.'

Stephano's words were like a douche of cold water to Helen. Her hands fell to her sides as Carlo turned back to his nephew, saying, 'Yes, of course, you're right.' Taking Helen by the hand, he led her into the house, explaining, 'Stephano brought bad news. Unfortunately, one of my oil tankers has suffered an explosion outside the port of La Plata, in the Argentine.' Reaching the bedroom, he swung round to face her, his expression grim. 'I have to go, Helena. There are some casualties, but the numbers aren't confirmed yet. As the owner of the line, it is my responsibility. I am flying out to Buenos Aires immediately to try and get the mess sorted out.'

Helen felt ashamed of her own selfish thoughts. For a moment, when Stephano had mentioned Carlo leaving, she had imagined that was why Carlo was behaving so tenderly towards her, simply for his nephew's benefit, when he knew he was going away. She was disgusted with herself as, once again, she realised how little she knew of this man who was her husband, how great was his responsibility to the people who worked for him and, surprisingly, how much he obviously cared. She could see it in the worried frown that marred his handsome face, and her softly voiced, 'I am sorry, Carlo. How terrible!' sounded grossly inadequate. Little did she know, that the moisture in the huge green eyes, fixed on her husband's face, told him more clearly than words how she felt.

'Not to worry, *cara*. I will be back as soon as I can.' Raising one hand, he gently stroked down her cheek. 'I will call when I have time, and I want you to promise me you will stay here until I return,' he demanded softly.

'Yes. Yes, I will.'

'Good. You and I still have to have a talk, but now there is no time,' he opined, adding, 'I want you to forget all about the past, and just concentrate on last night, hmmm?' Dropping a swift kiss on her brow, he swung round and disappeared into the bathroom.

CHAPTER TEN

HELEN stood on the drive until the Mercedes had vanished, then slowly turned and made her way back into the villa. The last twenty-four hours had left Helen emotionally drained. Carlo's lovemaking of the previous night and her own uninhibited response, followed by the realisation that she loved her arrogant, cynical husband, had deprived her of the ability to think straight, and his tender concern this morning only confused her more.

It was the evening news on TV, that finally brought her back to reality. She sat up abruptly as the newscaster described in detail the fire on board an oil tanker, anchored off the port of La Plata. Two casualties had been reported, experts were being called in to deal with the resultant oil slick, and the president of the company was already on his way to the scene. She found it hard to relate the words or pictures to her husband, and, hearing Sophia calling, she switched off the set and went downstairs.

The days merged into a week, and Helen had come no nearer to sorting out her feelings, or what she intended to do about her newfound love for her absent husband. Somehow the villa seemed empty, even lonely, the evenings long, and dinner a dreary meal without his abrasive presence, the solitary nights worse...

There had been no word from Carlo, only a brief message from Stephano saying Carlo was fine, but very busy, and she was to look after herself. It had hurt to think he had time to call Stephano in London, but not his wife.

It was with a heavy heart that she climbed into bed on the Saturday night. Sleep was a long time in coming as she tossed and turned restlessly; the bed had never seemed so large when Carlo shared it with her. She had toyed with the idea of going back to her old room, but quickly dismissed it. Just to lie in the bed they had shared was a kind of comfort—remembering his hard body entwined with her own fed the fierce hunger of her love for him.

Helen awoke with a start; the phone's ringing shocked her out of a troubled sleep. In her haste to answer it, she nearly knocked it off the bedside table. Shooting a quick glance at the clock she realised it was four in the morning. Immediately she feared the worst; something had happened to Carlo or Gran! With a pounding heart, she raised the receiver.

'*Pronto*, Helen speaking.'

'*Cara mia*, how are you?' It was Carlo's voice, she almost dropped the phone again, her hand was trembling so much.

'Carlo, where are you?' she responded breathlessly. 'What are you doing? Are you all right? Why are you calling?'—a dozen things she wanted to ask him.

'*Whoa*, one at a time, Helena.' She could hear the amusement in his voice, the line surprisingly clear. 'I am still in Buenos Aires, and I didn't get a chance to call earlier. There is a damn strike on here. I have had this call booked for days. I thought I might be back this weekend, but it looks as if it will take at least another week, maybe more to get things sorted out. But enough of my problems. What have you been doing to amuse yourself?' he questioned hardily.

The reaction at hearing his voice and knowing he was all right made Helen reply angrily, 'Do you realise it's four in the morning? I was asleep, what else would I be doing in the middle of the night?' Deep laughter greeted her comment.

'I'm sorry, *cara*, I forgot about the time difference. I've only just finished a late dinner, and as for the rest, if I was there I could show you,' he drawled sexily.

Her stomach clenched with a shaft of longing so intense she almost groaned out loud. 'Well, yes, but——,' she got out before Carlo interrupted her.

'God, Helena, I have a vivid picture in my head of the last fantastic night we were together,' he groaned. 'The thought of you in our bed makes me ache. Tell me, what are you wearing?'

An imp of mischief made her respond in a low, husky voice, dragging out each word, 'Well, at the moment, a gorgeous...golden...' she was sure she heard him moan as she continued, 'tan, and a generous spray of *Miss Dior*. Enough for you?' she asked sexily.

'Oh, Helena, what are you trying to do? Drive me out of my mind?'

'The thought never entered my head,' she lied, the thought of him never being out of her head for more than a couple of minutes at a time. 'But the idea is very appealing right now.'

'You have the worst timing of anyone I have ever met,' he derided. 'All suggestively submissive on terraces, or vineyards, and now, when I am at the other side of the world and can do nothing about it. I'm beginning to think you do it deliberately. Promise you will stay as you are until I return,' he demanded throatily.

Laughingly she replied, 'You're kidding! I'll freeze to death!'

'Don't worry, I will soon warm you up, *cara*.'

Helen's heart raced at his words, her breasts hardening to taut arousal, and it was all she could do to reply softly, 'All right, Carlo, but please don't be too long.' There was a long silence, then Carlo's voice, deep and warm. 'I will try not to be, *mia sposa*.'

She did not know if he heard her whispered, 'Goodnight, *caro*,' as the line went dead.

Helen slowly replaced the receiver, and slipped back down the bed. Hugging herself, she curled up cosily beneath the single cover, her mind clearer than it had been for weeks.

She loved Carlo totally; the sound of his voice alone
was enough to make her tremble with desire. She recalled the last words he had spoken before leaving for
the Argentine. He had told her to forget the past and
concentrate on the evening they had just spent together.
Surely that meant he wanted them to make a fresh start?
She hoped so.

Carlo was a proud man, and her family had treated
him badly. It was not surprising that he had wanted some
revenge, and the scar on his temple was a constant reminder. She could accept that, she loved her father
dearly, but no longer saw him as infallible. Her own attitude on meeting Carlo again had been a defence mech-
anism against her own feelings. She could see now that,
instead of trying to fight him, she should have tried to
reason things out, then Carlo perhaps would not have
been so coldly angry at times. She thought of the
weekends they had spent together, realising that when
she had managed to forget her burning resentment at
the way he had tricked her and the way he made her
feel, they got along remarkably well together, sharing
the same sense of humour, and many of the same
pastimes.

The chemical reaction between them was explosive,
and always had been since that very first day they met
in Rome. Whatever the reason he had for bringing her
here, he wanted her; even a man of his experience
couldn't fake his reactions so convincingly, and God
knew she wanted him. Surely a man who had a willing
and enthusiastic wife at home would not go looking for
any diversions? she told herself, smiling as she remembered their shared passion, but not for long—the memory
of their wedding night made her groan. He had said six
years . . . a slip of the tongue. Helen buried her head in
the pillow. She would not think about it, and she vowed
that when Carlo returned she would be exactly what he
wanted: an obedient, loving wife.

The next day Helen woke with a new sense of purpose and a much lighter heart. She determined to make a full inventory of what else needed to be done in the villa, and to try and have it all finished before Carlo returned. The house became a hive of activity, so much so that even Tommaso lost his perpetual solemn look, and smiled at his crazy women, as he called them.

The weather cooled slightly and made the work seem easier. Sophia and Helen flitted around, hanging curtains, pictures, moving furniture. By the following week there was little left to do, but Carlo had still not returned.

On the Thursday Helen decided to spend the morning by the pool. It would soon be too cold for sunbathing and, as she stretched out on the lounger, she felt reasonably content. Her hand gently stroked across her abdomen. She had not been to the doctor yet, but she was sure she was pregnant, she was eighteen days late with her period. Already her breasts felt fuller, but the deciding factor, she thought wryly, was her inability to eat *focaccia* anymore. Her favourite breakfast and she could not bear the sight of it! Of course, Sophia had noticed. Helen wondered what Carlo would say when she told him. She had watched him with Anna's children, and she had no doubt he would make a marvellous father, firm but fun...

Stephano's 'Hello, Aunty,' brought her out of her reverie. Sitting up, she turned to see him walking jauntily across the patio.

'If you call me Aunty one more time, Stephano, I'll hit you! It makes me feel about ninety!' she said indignantly. 'And what are you doing here? Is Carlo with you?' The thought made her heart beat faster as she swung her legs off the chair.

'No. He is still in the Argentine, but he managed to contact me in London yesterday. He said to tell you he will be back home on Saturday and would I check that you were all right? Satisfied?' he smirked cheekily.

'Well, almost. What time on Saturday, do you know?'
Two more days wasn't all that long to wait.

'Yes, he is flying into Rome late Friday night, and I
have booked him on the first plane to Sicily Saturday
morning. He should be here about lunch time.'

Something that had puzzled Helen when Carlo left
came back to her with Stephano's words.

'Why did you have to book a flight? What's the matter
with the plane we came across in? It was Carlo's, I remember you saying so at the time.

'Carlo sold it. Didn't he tell you?' Stephano asked,
surprised.

'But he loved flying his own plane.'

Helen recalled him telling her so, years ago, in one of
those rambling conversations they had shared.

'Yes, well, he does, but unfortunately, he failed the
physical a while back, and had his licence revoked.'

Helen paled under her tan, dreading what she might
hear. 'But why? There's nothing wrong with him!' Wild
thoughts of some dread disease chased through her mind.
'Or is there? Tell me! You must tell me, Stephano!' Her
hand gripped his arm in her panic.

'Hey, hold on, Helen, it is nothing serious—just his
eyesight is not what it was.'

Taking a deep breath, she said, 'I didn't know there
was any thing the matter with his eyes.' The relief that
it was nothing more serious subdued her panic.

'There wasn't until he had the accident a couple of
years ago and got that cut over his temple. It affected
the optic nerve, apparently. He had a few operations,
but about six months ago the doctors told him that was
it. There was nothing more they could do, so he has only
partial sight in one eye, and who wants a one-eyed pilot?'
he laughed.

Helen did not know how she got through the rest of
Stephano's visit. He made a few attempts to cheer her
up with the news from England about the staff in the

office, but, sensing how disturbed she was, after a few more desultory comments he gave up trying and left.

She went straight to their bedroom and, flinging herself on the bed, cried her heart out. No wonder Carlo had been so furious! It was bad enough knowing she was indirectly responsible for his accident, but this latest revelation was a hundred times worse. She was overcome with guilt and wished futilely that she could turn the clock back. How could she ever hope he would forgive her?

She eventually dragged herself off the bed and made her way into the bathroom. After a quick shower, she dressed in a simple shirtwaister—she had to meet Anna after lunch—and went downstairs. Over a solitary meal she convinced herself that although it had been a great shock to her, finding out about his impaired eyesight, it didn't really change anything. Because Carlo had known all along, and yet in the past few weeks he had shown her that he was capable of caring for her. She had to believe, for her own peace of mind, because she loved him, that this new considerate, indulgent man was the true Carlo.

By the time she met Anna and Selina for the weekly trip to the hospital, she had convinced herself that everything would work out all right, and she was feeling much more confident.

Anna had confided to her that Selina was suffering from a complicated blood disorder, but they hoped it was now under control. Unfortunately, this week's visit turned out to be not quite so routine.

They waited in the small, rather miserable side room while Selina was taken away for a few simple blood tests. On the other occasions, when Helen had come along, it had not taken more than half an hour, but today, an hour passed with still no sign of Selina reappearing. Anna was trying her best to look unconcerned, but Helen could sense that the other girl was worried. Helen was worried herself, but determinedly engaged Anna in conversation, talking about the house, Gran and Andrea, anything to try and divert Anna.

It was no good, another half-hour passed with still no sign of Selina. Helen suggested she go and try to find someone who could tell them what the delay was, and was just about to do so when Selina's doctor walked in. Doctor Alberti was a lovely man, small and rather plump, with the kindest brown eyes and an engaging smile, but today there was no sign of his usual grin and he looked forbiddingly serious.

Gently, he explained. Selina was haemorrhaging internally, he suspected the child had been for some time, and he was unable to say, at the moment, how it had happened. They had taken her into theatre and would try to stem the flow, and hopefully after a few days in intensive care she should be all right again, and her condition could again be stabilised. Anna was distraught, and it didn't help that her husband was at the other side of the world on business in Sydney. Helen did her best to persuade her everything would be fine, but she felt woefully inadequate at the job. Time seemed to stand still, each minute as long as an hour. Helen went out and found them some coffee but it didn't help much, and when, some three hours later, the doctor returned, both women jumped to their feet. The news was good, the operation was a success, and hopefully Selina would not need to spend much more than a week in hospital. Tears flooded Helen's eyes, and when she turned to Anna they were reflected in hers. Helplessly they clung to each other, crying and laughing at the same time.

The sight of Selina lying in an over-large hospital bed in intensive care, looking almost as white as the pillow she rested on, with a drip attached to her arm, had a profound effect on Helen. Her hand automatically went to her stomach, to the life she was sure was growing there, and she finally saw how utterly impossible it would be to leave a child of her own, as she had so casually proposed to Carlo. She heard again his comment, that she did not understand herself. How right he was! He had agreed to her condition so quickly, because he knew her well enough to know that she was not the type of woman who could leave her child. His sensitivity filled her with a deep sense of shame and disgust at her own childishness.

It was Friday evening before Anna and Helen left the hospital. The night before they had spent in a room provided by the hospital. Helen had called Tommaso, and he had brought them some toilet articles and a huge food hamper with two flasks of coffee, courtesy of Sophia, bless her. Anna had managed to get in touch with her husband, but Aldo reckoned the quickest he could make it back from Sydney would be Saturday. The neighbour who had collected the boys from school offered to keep them at her house as soon as Anna told her what had happened, so that had been one less worry for Anna.

It was late before Helen finally got back to the villa, having seen Anna safely back home. She was exhausted, and Sophia's message that she had just missed Carlo calling did nothing for her flagging spirits, until Sophia gave her the number and added he had called from Rome, and would be home in the morning. It was eight o'clock, and Helen decided he would probably have gone out for dinner. She would have a bath and something to eat before ringing him.

Replete with good food, and comfortably ensconced in bed, Helen picked up the phone, and cheerfully dialled the Rome number.

At first she was not surprised by the feminine voice that answered the phone, imagining it was the hotel receptionist. Until, having asked for Signor Manzitti's room number, she heard the lady reply, 'Why, Helen, didn't you know? This is Carlo's apartment.'

It was Caterina. Helen doubled over in pain; she felt as if a knife had slashed her heart, splitting it open so that agony poured out. All her wishful dreams of the past weeks were scattered like so many leaves in the wind.

Biting her lip to hold back the sob that rose in her throat, she forced herself to respond politely, and ask again for Carlo. He loved little Selina, he was entitled to know she was ill, even if he was with his mistress. But Caterina's mockingly drawled, 'I'm sorry, Helen, he isn't available right now. Shall I tell him to call you?' was too much for Helen and the receiver fell from her lifeless hand.

Long afterwards, Helen could never remember how she got through that night. She cried and cried until, exhausted, she fell asleep. But her dreams were haunted by visions of Carlo and Caterina in each other's arms. The thought of her husband making love to another woman had her crying even in her sleep, and when she woke the next morning she was a different girl altogether.

She felt as if she had aged a decade overnight. She had to drag herself into the shower, the jets of warm water over her naked flesh doing nothing to soothe the aching pain, the searing jealousy that the thought of Carlo with Caterina evoked. She dressed carefully in a white shirtwaister and matching white sandals. Methodily, she brushed her long hair till it gleamed, flicking it carelessly behind her ears. Her make-up took longer, but nothing could disguise completely the puffiness around her eyes so, taking her sunglasses, she put them on and made her way downstairs. Calling to Sophia that she would like her breakfast on the patio, she slowly made her way outside.

It was a beautiful day, the sun brilliant in a clear blue sky, a slight breeze off the sea keeping the temperature down. She loved this place, and could have been so happy here, if only Carlo had loved her. Helen felt the tears come to her eyes and swallowed hard, choking them back. Her surroundings held no pleasure for her now, and she was flooded with an overpowering home-sickness for the people she was used to: Gran and Andrea, Joe and Martha. She longed passionately to return to England. If she could make it through today, face Carlo without breaking down, it would be all right, she told herself. Fleetingly, it crossed her mind to be the obedient Sicilian wife he had demanded, but deep in her heart, she knew it would never work. Helen was not the stuff that martyrs were made of; she had too much pride. She was a survivor, she would fulfil her part of their bargain to the letter, then leave, no matter what it cost her in personal anguish.

Lunch time came and went, with no sign of Carlo. Tommaso had left at twelve to pick him up at the airport, but it was four in the afternoon before the sound of the car pulling up outside alerted Helen to her husband's arrival. She was glad of the delay, as it had given her a chance to come to terms with his betrayal, and feed the cold knot of anger that had taken root inside her.

Safely ensconced in the family room, she found that her pulse-rate quickened as she heard him pounding up the stairs, and go into their bedroom. A hollow laugh escaped her. My God! The supreme egotist, did he really believe she would be lying in the bed, waiting for him? She heard him calling 'Helena,' and was surprised at how normal her own voice sounded, as she replied, 'Up here, Carlo.'

It took every ounce of willpower she possessed to remain seated as he strode into the room, her every instinct crying out for her to throw herself into his arms. She need not have bothered, as he strolled across the room and pulled her straight out of the chair and into his arms, his mouth closing over hers in a hungry kiss. She clamped her lips together and forced herself to remain unresponsive in his hold.

Sensing her resistance, Carlo lifted his head, and held her away from him, his dark eyes searching her own.

'What's wrong, Helena?' he asked, obviously puzzled. Bravely she held his gaze, her face expressionless. 'Nothing's wrong. What should be?' she questioned in turn. She watched as his eyes widened, still curious, the mockery she had expected not there. Evidently Caterina had not told him about the phone call, and he was playing the part of the caring husband. The thought fed the fire of her anger, making it easier for her to face him.

Carlo frowned heavily. 'You've been crying, *cara*. Come, you can tell me.' Then magically his frown cleared. 'But of course—Selina. Sophia mentioned she was in hospital; no wonder you're upset. How stupid of me to forget. Tell me, how is she?' he queried gently, his arms tightening around her comfortingly.

Helen leapt at the excuse. 'I spoke to Anna this morning. Selina is much better and has been transferred to an ordinary ward.' She felt guilty at using the child's illness to disguise her own distress, but Carlo's nearness was playing havoc with her senses. Lifting slender hands to his chest, she carefully eased out of his hold. His grip tightened for an instant, then she was free. Looking somewhere over his shoulder, she continued, 'Aldo is due back today, and I promised we would visit the hospital this evening, then have dinner with them later. I'll get you something to eat now, you must be hungry,' she rattled on, moving to slide past him as she spoke, but it was not to be so easy. Strong fingers fastened around her wrist, and she swung back into his arms.

'Not so fast, *cara*,' he commanded, his hand caressing her throat, tipping her face up to his. His dark eyes kindled with a mixture of amusement and desire as he lowered his head to hers. He was going to kiss her, and for a second Helen thought, why not? God knows she wanted him! But the sound of Caterina's voice ringing in her head squashed the thought.

'I'll get your food,' she muttered, turning so his mouth grazed her cheek.

'Ah, Helena,' he whispered, nuzzling her ear. 'I am not hungry for food. It is a much more basic appetite I need filling, and you know it, *mia sposa*.'

She stiffened in his hold, her hands once again pushing him away. How dared he? The conceit of the man, when she knew that not a dozen hours ago, he had been in another woman's bed! She was just about to confront him with the fact, when he took a step back, the better to watch her.

'It's not just Selina. Something else is bothering you,' he decided, finally aware that she was not responding as he wished. 'So, Helena, are you going to tell me?' he demanded, his handsome face hardening at her reticence. Gathering every shred of willpower she possessed and trying to ignore the hand moving soothingly on her back, she met his gaze defiantly, and in a cold voice told him, 'I am pregnant.'

His eyes blazed with a triumphant delight and that, more than anything, gave Helen the strength to continue, 'I suggest from now on, you get one of your lady friends to satisfy your basic desires. According to our agreement, I am no longer obliged to.'

Carlo's reaction to her statement was as odd as it was unexpected. Helen had thought he would be angry; instead, he turned and walked the length of the room and back, eventually settling his long frame in the chair Helen had so recently vacated. He raised one hand to his face, and with thumb and forefinger rubbed his eyes. Suddenly he looked tired, almost exhausted. She stared at him, noting the lines of tiredness etched into his brown skin, and when his hand dropped from his face, she was trapped and held by the expression in his dark eyes. For an instant she thought she saw pain reflected there. Remorse flooded through her as she recalled Stephano's information about Carlo's eyesight. She took a step forward involuntarily. She ached to go to him and beg his forgiveness, but as she moved he spoke, quickly disabusing her of the notion.

'So that is the reason for my less than exuberant welcome,' he drawled sarcastically. 'You are pregnant, at least, you imagine you are. Tell me, is it confirmed?'

'No, of course it isn't, not yet, but I am almost three weeks late.' She added some sarcasm of her own. 'I can hardly pop across to my family doctor, as you well know. You still have my passport,' she ended truculently.

'Now, now, Helena, don't get excited.' Lazily he laid his head back against the high-backed leather chair, cynically eyeing her slender form. 'If what you say is true, it can't be good for you.'

'Good for me!' she exclaimed. Was that all he had to say? He sat there looking as cool as a cucumber, not in the least perturbed by her revelation, and she was loath to admit, she was peeved by his reaction, or lack of it.

'It is the rest of your statement that interests me. Am I to understand that now you are pregnant, you imagine you have fulfilled your part of the bargain?' he asked.

'Yes.'

'I see.' His heavy-lidded eyes half closed, hiding his expression. 'And if I wish to indulge my—what was it you said? Ah, yes, my basic appetites, I should do so with someone other than you, my wife?'

'Got it in one, how astute of you,' she responded flippantly, in an effort to mask her true feelings. The thought of him with another woman chilled the blood in her veins, but she had chosen her path, and had to stick to it. She had too much pride to share his favours.

'Are you sure that is what you want, Helena?' No, no that wasn't what she wanted, the words screamed in her head, but she dared not voice them.

'Yes, that's exactly what I want.' The lie nearly stuck in her throat, and his coolly voiced, 'So be it,' had her mouth dropping open in amazement.

So that was it, no remonstrations, but a cold acceptance. What had she expected—an avowal of undying love, and her husband pleading for her favours? Some chance, with the sexy Caterina ever-willing, she thought bitterly.

So it was all the more surprising when Carlo rose from the seat and moved to stand in front of her. She knew she should turn and go, but she could not make her legs move. His strong hands curved gently over her shoulders, his touch sending a tremor down the length of her body. She stared up at him, unable to fathom the brooding look in his dark eyes.

'Just one question, *cara*.'

'Yes?' she queried. 'What is it?'

'Tell me, where has the woman gone whom I spoke to on the telephone? The woman who shared my bed the last night I was here, and turned it into paradise?'

Helen's heart turned over at his words, and words of love rose in her throat, but were never uttered, as he continued, a hard edge to his tone, 'The woman I worked twenty hours a day to get back to, only to find she had vanished,' he snarled, all trace of tenderness gone, as his fingers dug into her flesh.

Helplessly she swayed towards him, his touch, his scent seducing her, until she remembered the anguish of the previous night. Never again, she vowed, and, dropping her eyes, she muttered, 'I don't understand what you're talking about,' adding in an abrupt attempt to change the subject, 'We'd better hurry if we are going to see Selina.'

Carlo almost threw her away from him, his fury hitting her like an arctic blast.

'By all means let us go and see Selina,' he bit out. 'My God! You "don't understand",' he mimicked her own cool words viciously. 'That is your trouble, Helena, you never have understood, never wanted to.' His black eyes raked her from head to toe, stripping her with a glance. 'My God, you have the body of a woman, and the sensual appetites of one, as I know too well, but the mind of a child. If you ever decide to grow up, let me know. I have wasted enough of my time already.'

Helen flinched under his tirade, not really following his reasoning, but furious at being called a child. He had made sure she wasn't, she thought bitterly, and in her fury she replied nastily, 'It is a pity you didn't come to that conclusion before you married me. You should have stuck to Caterina. She is obviously more your style.'

Carlo's lips curved in a knowing smile. 'Perhaps you are right. At least Caterina is one hundred per cent woman and not afraid to show it. It would do you no harm to take a few lessons from her,' he opined silkily, before turning to stride to the door. Stopping, he swung back to face Helen. 'One more thing, Helena. You will still share my bed.'

Her eyes widened in horror. 'You're joking,' she spluttered, astounded at the cheek of the man.

'It is no joke, *mia sposa*. You have made a fool of me once too often, but never again. I will not have Sophia gossiping all over the place that my wife left my bed within weeks, understand?' he demanded harshly.

'What is the matter, Carlo, frightened people may question your virility?' she mocked. 'Well, too bad, because I won't.'

'Oh, but you will,' he interrupted, moving catlike to stand close to her, his black eyes blazing into hers. 'Don't worry, I won't ask anything of you, I don't think I could bear to touch you, the way I feel right now. As for questioning my virility, there will be no doubt...' Insolently he ran his hand over her belly. 'You are walking proof of that,' he mocked.

She blushed scarlet at his words, but could not stop the tremor that coursed through her, as his hand stroked lower to her thighs, then pushed her firmly away.

'Oh no, Helena, I am tired of your games. What was the word you used?' he drawled derisively, fully aware of how his touch had affected her. 'If your *basic* appetites need feeding, you will have to get on your knees and beg, and I might just oblige.' And, swinging on his heel, he walked out, slamming the door behind him.

Helen sank gratefully into the large chair, her legs trembling. He had left, but it was no comfort to her. She had thought she had seen all his moods, but this was something else. She still could not sort out in her head exactly what he had meant, but she was too emotionally drained to try. She should be congratulating herself; she had alienated him for good, this time. It had been there in his eyes as he turned and left the room, so why was it that all she felt was a numbing, cold despair?

Later, after a quick shower and change, Helen joined Carlo in the *salone*, where Sophia served them with coffee and sandwiches, fussing over Carlo as if he had been gone three months, rather than three weeks.

He made no attempt at conversation, and when Helen tentatively suggested it was time they left for the hospital, the contemptuous look, and his icily polite response had her nerves stretched to breaking point. Poor Sophia, busily clearing the dishes, could be in no doubt that something was seriously wrong between them.

Aldo and Anna were at the hospital when they arrived, and were delighted to see them. Selina appeared to be much better, her eyes lighting up when she recognised her Uncle Carlo, and he was a changed man in the little girl's company, his smile warm and tender, his patience with her childish questions seemingly inexhaustible.

Aldo took them to a private club for dinner, having arranged earlier for a table. Anna was looking and feeling much better than when Helen had last seen her, and they chattered quite pleasantly while the meal was served. Unfortunately, to Helen's chagrin, Carlo continued in the same icy vein as earlier, and it was soon obvious to their friends that something was wrong. As the night wore on, Carlo gave up even bothering to be so polite. Every remark Helen made he treated with biting sarcasm and, after one particularly vicious comment, she could stand it no longer, and excused herself to go to the powder room. Anna immediately followed her, her first words being, 'Come on, Helen, tell me what is wrong.'

To Helen's horror, her eyes flooded with tears, and she broke down completely, sobbing her heart out on Anna's shoulder, her last reserves of self-control swept away. Between sobs, she found herself telling Anna the

whole story, from the first day she had met Carlo in
Rome. Somehow, confiding in someone else eased the
ache in her heart, and stopped her tears, but she was
not prepared for Anna's reaction, which was to burst
out laughing.

'Oh, Helen, what a fool you are! Carlo would never
marry for revenge; his father might, but Carlo, never. I
have known him for years, he is a shrewd businessman,
but a true romantic at heart. Good heavens, girl, he loves
you. It is there in his eyes for the world to see every time
he looks at you, and that is most of the time.'

Helen was stunned by Anna's reaction, but when she
thought about it, she saw a vivid picture in her mind's
eye of a red rose in a coffee mug, a helicopter ride for
her pleasure, a house he wanted to name after her.
Perhaps Anna was right. The first faint glimmer of hope
lightened her heart. Was it possible Carlo loved her, had
done all along? In Rome she had been utterly convinced
of his love, at first. Wasn't it La Rochefoucauld who
said, 'When one loves, one doubts even what one most
believes.'? How very true, she thought.

Anna was speaking again. 'Take some advice from an
old married lady. You do love him?'

Helen could deny it no longer. 'Oh, yes, I always have.'

'Then get out there and tell him, before the night's
over.'

It wouldn't be easy, and then Helen remembered
Caterina, and found herself telling Anna all about the
phone call last night.

'Whatever Caterina was doing in Carlo's apartment
last night, Diego would be doing it with her. They got
married yesterday, and it was arranged at the party the
other week that they would borrow Carlo's apartment.
You idiot, Helen! Carlo wasn't to know he would need
it himself. If you ask him, you'll find he probably spent
the night in a hotel.'

Helen felt as if a great weight had been lifted from
her, and a smile of pure joy lit his face. 'Anna, I'm so

glad I talked to you, I feel heaps better. I can never thank you enough!'

'Don't thank me, just make sure you get things straight with that husband of yours. Now come on and fix your face, and let's get back to the men before they think we have left them.'

Helen was happy to follow Anna's advice, and quickly they made their way back to the table.

Catching Carlo's eyes on her, she gave him a tentative smile, determined to try and put things right between them, but he froze her with a look of such disdain, she cringed with embarrassment. Knowing he had not been unfaithful with Caterina might make her feel a whole lot better, but she was left with the problem of how to convince Carlo she loved him, and, more to the point, trying to persuade him to love her was not going to be easy, especially after the scene this afternoon.

The evening limped along and the relief was unanimous when Carlo suggested they call it a night, his excuse being that he was tired from all the travelling, and he knew they would understand. The drive home was completed in silence. Helen cast a sidelong glance at her husband, and what she saw in his face gave her no hope at all; for all the notice he took of her, she might as well have been a stranger.

Following him into the villa, she went straight upstairs as Carlo turned into his study without a word being spoken. Entering the bedroom, she kicked off her shoes, and slipped out of her dress, heading straight for the bathroom. The sharp needle-spray of the shower was soothing to her troubled mind, and gradually her head cleared, bringing the past into sharp focus, as never before.

From the first day she had met Carlo she had fallen head over heels in love with him. From their first kiss, she would willingly have gone to bed with him, her moral upbringing forgotten in the flame of sensual awakening he ignited in her. Looking back she could see that it had been Carlo who had always called a halt to their love-making, while she had barely been able to keep her hands off him. He had insisted they get married, and that he must ask her father for permission. It was Carlo who wanted everything done correctly, and he had cared enough about her to slow things down when they threatened to get out of hand. The last day, when they were naked by the pool, Helen had begged to be his completely, and even then he had managed to restrain himself from actually taking her virginity.

Her father coming home early, and soundly denouncing Carlo, had been a shock to Helen that she had not had time to assimilate. The last week she had been existing on a highly emotional plane, and when she heard her father's story, the only thought that registered was that the man she loved beyond anything had deceived her. It never occurred to her to question what her father said; she trusted him. Carlo was not what she had thought, and belatedly she remembered her moral up-bringing, and was flooded with shame and guilt. In retrospect she could see how wrong she had been. There could be no love without trust, and she had not trusted Carlo. Perhaps at eighteen she had been too young to recognise that fact.

Carlo had never lied to her. The knowledge that he was wealthy had been there for her to see. His beautiful clothes, his flitting back and forwards across the country by air, expensive cars, should have told her. He had certainly not tried to hide his wealth, and as for his engagement to Maria, it was not so surprising he did not mention it. It had been years before, and obviously he had not thought it important. His relationship with Maria had been that of old friends, and anyway, the few times Helen and Carlo met they had been far too engrossed in each other to get around to discussing family histories. He had freely admitted his father's involvement in the cancellation of her father's work permit, but added it had been none of his doing and he could do nothing about it.

Helen groaned in self-derision as, turning off the tap, she wrapped a large bath towel around her slender body, and went back into the bedroom. She had repaid his honesty by running away. No wonder he thought she was childish. He was right. She should at least have listened to his explanation.

Smiling wryly at her reflection in the dressing-table mirror, she wondered how she could have been so stupid. Even worse, meeting him again two years later, she had behaved just as childishly as before, determined to think the worst of him. He had been angry, true, but he did have some reason and the fiasco of their wedding night had been her own fault. All willing submission, then screaming at him like a fishwife.

Apart from their first night, he had not treated her badly, quite the opposite, in fact. When they made love he was a gentle, considerate partner, always making sure of her pleasure before his own, even though she had tried to make it as difficult for him as she could.

Their last night together, when she had finally given up trying to resist him, touching him, loving him, had been marvellous. They had spent the night glorying in each other's pleasure. The next day, when she had been wary of so much as looking at him, frightened in case she saw him gloating at her surrender, he had amazed her by being the caring, considerate man she remembered of old. His concern had lasted all the time he was away. It was still there in his eyes when he had walked into the room this afternoon, and swept her into his arms. Then she'd had to spoil everything by insisting on the stupid bargain they had made. Rejecting him, simply because of Caterina and her vicious tongue.

Sighing deeply Helen opened the dresser drawer. It was no use blaming Caterina, hadn't Carlo told her himself that the lady was not his mistress? And he did not lie. But still she had been prepared to believe anyone rather than him. The mess she was in was of her own making. Trust, that was what it was all about, and so far she had shown none at all. All the soul-searching in the world was not going to make things right between her and her husband. It was up to her to do something positive to improve things, but what...

Her eyes fell on a flash of red—the teddy Carlo had given her. Dare she...? A flush rose in her cheeks at the idea, then quickly she picked it up, before she could change her mind, and held it in front of her. Well, why not? She had nothing to lose but her pride, and everything to gain if Anna was right and Carlo did care for her. She was not asking for his love straight away, but surely it might come with time. Perhaps she could persuade Carlo she was enough woman for him. He had called her a child and told her she did not understand, and he had been right. Now it was up to her to prove she had grown into a mature woman.

Helen surveyed her reflection in the mirror, and blushed as red as the slip of silk she was wearing. Fastening the small studs between her legs did nothing to improve the image, only pulling the front lower, so the fine lace barely covered her nipples. A deep V slashed almost to her navel gaped open until she pulled the neatly threaded laces together in a small bow between her breasts. That did not improve the image much, only accentuating her cleavage. Ruefully she turned sideways, and almost ripped the thing off. The silk, cut away at the sides to her waist, revealed the soft curve of her buttocks, and the fine spaghetti straps, curving over her shoulders, didn't look capable of supporting anything. It was much more suggestive than she had realised, and wondered what possible use it was. Then grinned. Hadn't she found a use for it...

Turning, she walked barefoot across the room and out through the open windows on to the terrace. Leaning against the balustrade, she drank in the cool beauty of the night. With only the sounds of the sea, and the moon and stars for company, she smiled softly to herself, her own troubles insignificant in the stillness and tranquillity of the late September night. She did not feel cold; the sea breeze caressed her burning skin, relieving all her tension. She was happy. It was so simple, she loved Carlo and would tell him so. Gently she stroked her flat stomach in wonder. His child was already growing inside her, safe and loved. She laughed out loud, suddenly supremely confident, the happy sound echoing on the night air. It was their child; how foolish she had been to think she would ever leave it.

'Tell me, what is so amusing?' a deep voice challenged.

CHAPTER ELEVEN

SLOWLY Helen turned. She felt the breath still in her chest as she looked at Carlo. He was standing in the open window, the light from the room behind outlining his large frame. As her eyes grew accustomed to the gloom, she noticed he was wearing a short black towelling robe, and somehow he appeared dark and forbidding. She took a step towards him. 'Carlo,' she said, then halted, one glance at his icy countenance, chilling her.

'Tell me, Helena, what are you trying to do? Catch pneumonia? Surely having to share my bed can't be that bad?' he derided, his dark eyes skimming over her near-naked form.

'Oh, no, no!' she cried; how could he think such a thing when the opposite was true? Moving to stand in front of him, she bravely stared up at his harsh face, 'I—I—just—I wanted to think,' she ended lamely.

Taking her by the arm, Carlo roughly pushed her back into the bedroom, saying, 'For the sake of our unborn child, I suggest you do your thinking indoors in future, especially if you intend to go around half-naked.' He followed her inside.

It wasn't going at all as she had planned, and in one last-ditch effort, she turned and reached out to him as he would have walked past her, her hand catching the front of his robe. He stopped in mid-stride, and looked down first at her hand, then up to her face.

'Was there something you wanted?' he questioned silkily, his glance flicking suggestively down over her breasts, which were clearly displayed beneath the minute covering of silk. Slowly his hand lifted, and with one finger he carefully traced the outline of red lace. Helen's response was immediate and uncontrollable, her breasts hardening, the taut nipples straining against the soft material. She gazed up at him, her eyes brilliant in her flushed face. She could tell nothing of what he was thinking, and the effect of his closeness, that electric awareness she felt in his company, was fast spiralling out of control. A soft sigh escaped her, and, casting aside all restraint, she responded huskily, 'Yes, I want you.'

Carlo slid his fingers under the small bow between her breasts, and gently tugged. 'So, that is what this is for.' His tight lips twisted cynically. 'This afternoon you could not bear me to touch you. Something about satisfying my baser instincts elsewhere, I recall. Tell me, what made you change your mind?' he queried coldly.

He wasn't making it easy for her, and for a second she thought of running, but she had done that too often in the past. Her fingers curled tensely in the soft fabric of his robe, her knuckles brushing against the fine hair on his chest, sending a frisson of pleasure up her arm. This was the moment of truth. What she said now could affect her whole life, and the knowledge made her voice shake.

'This afternoon I—I was upset. I did not sleep well,' was the nearest she could get to mentioning Caterina, 'and with realising I was pregnant, and your arriving hours late, I wasn't thinking straight.' His fingers lazily untied the red bow as she spoke, and she gulped as his hands curved slowly under her firm breasts, cupping them in his palms, the teddy slipping unnoticed to her waist.

'I'm sorry, I didn't mean what I said,' she got out, before swaying towards him, her hands burrowing under his robe, stroking up to his broad shoulders, loving the feel of his naked flesh. Raising her head, so the light from the table lamp shone full on her lovely face, she blinked rapidly, in surprise, as Carlo eased her away from him.

Her attempt at seduction wasn't having much succcess, if the grim look in his eyes was anything to go by.

'So I am supposed to say OK, and take you to my bed. That is the scenario?' he asked sarcastically, not in the least affected by the half-naked woman before him, while Helen was a quivering mass of nerves. Still, she could not give up now.

'Yes, please,' she whispered throatily, straining towards him, her lips brushing the base of his throat.

'Why?' he bit out.

Helen could feel the tension in him, as she closed the gap between them. Pressing up against his unyielding frame, she whispered against his skin, 'Because I love you. I think I always have.' And with the admission made, she slid her arms completely around his neck, burying her head in his shoulder, afraid to look at him, amazed at her own audacity.

Violently her head was pulled back, Carlo's other hand leaving her breast, to clasp her firmly around the waist.

'Do you know what you are saying, or is this another one of your games?' he demanded bluntly.

Though his words were cold, Helen could feel his body stirring against her, and elation flooded her mind. It was there for him to see in the green eyes blazing into his. No longer shy, she was suddenly all woman, sensuous, teasing. Her mouth opened over the strong cord of his neck, her tongue licking lightly down to the pulse that beat in the base of his throat, and huskily she answered, 'No more games, Carlo. I love you.' Her fingers streaked through the black curly hair, urgently clasping his skull. 'I want you, in me, around me, over me, any way I can have you,' she answered, holding him, willing Carlo to recognize the truth of her words.

His arms tightened around her, moulding them together from shoulder to thigh. She watched in wonder as his expression softened his hard mouth, curved up at the corners in a slow smile. Fascinated, she touched her lips to his, and his mouth opened encouragingly beneath hers. Her tongue flicked out to explore the moist, dark cavern of his mouth, then subtly Carlo took over, the seducer becoming the seduced, as the kiss went on and on and on. Feverishly Helen caressed his dark head, while her heartbeats accelerated like a high-speed train, as achingly she writhed against him, wanting much more.

At last they drew apart, needing to breathe. Carlo, his eyes glittering wickedly triumphant, said, 'I think you should show me some of this love you mentioned, *cara*,' and swinging Helen up in his arms, he carried her to the bed, laying her down and removing the red teddy in one swift movement. Then, quickly shrugging off his robe, he joined her. As he knelt over her, his powerful hands moved gently down her body, like a sculptor molding her form, lingering at hip and thigh, long fingers pressing, stroking, then slowly feeling their way back up to cup her full breasts, thumbs waywardly teasing the rigid, dusky peaks.

Helen closed her eyes, breathing deeply, as waves of pleasure washed over her. Carlo's throatily voiced, 'So show me, touch me,' his hands holding her firmly to the bed, waiting, had her eyes flying open. She had forgotten she was supposed to be seducing him.

A mischievous smile parted her full lips and, rising up, she pushed Carlo over on to his back beside her. Balancing on one hand, she let her gaze travel suggestively over his gloriously naked body before she spoke.

'Certainly, *caro*,' she drawled. 'Where would you like me to start?' she queried, letting her other hand stroke down from his broad chest following the line of soft body hair to his navel, and lower to the light dusting of hair on his muscular thighs. Bending her head, her breasts tingling at the contact with his chest, she lightly licked over a hard male nipple, while her fingers edged slowly over his thigh to tangle in the thicker hair of his groin. She felt his muscles clench as he fought for control, and, raising her head, she grinned knowingly down at him. A chuckle escaped her.

At the sound of her chuckle, Carlo was lost. 'Oh, God!' he groaned. 'You're driving me crazy, Helena!'

Helen's last truly conscious thought was, he didn't take much seducing. Then Carlo's arms closed around her, and in seconds their positions were reversed. She glimpsed the naked desire in the depths of his dark eyes before his mouth closed over hers, blotting out everything, except the sensations his kiss aroused in her. She lost all sense of self, her lips clinging to his, while her hands sensuously travelled over every muscle and sinew of his broad back.

White-hot heat consumed them both as they explored, extorted, indulged in a wildly erotic feast of love.

Carlo's mouth tugged at the hardened tip of her breast, as his long fingers played between her thighs with deadly intent. Helen made no attempt to conceal her responses. Her legs thrashed wildly on the bed, as her hands slid down to his buttocks, her fingers digging into his flesh.

'Please, Carlo, now, now...' she moaned. She was drowning in desire, every nerve-end on fire, moist and throbbing for him, so Carlo's 'No' barely registered, but his stillness did. Dazedly she opened her eyes, unable to believe he could stop now. His black hair, damp with sweat, lay flat on his brow, a dull red flush stained his cheekbones, heightening the harsh planes of his face.

'Before I take you, I want your promise,' he rasped. 'Everything you vowed in church you will keep. No more stupid bargains.' His voice hoarse, he demanded, 'Say it, Helena, or I leave this bed now, for good.'

Helen could feel the iron tension in his body, and although passion glazed her huge green eyes, for an instant she saw and recognised a flash of vulnerability in Carlo's face. Her heart cried for him; this magnificent male animal, her husband, still did not believe her avowal of love. 'I promise, Carlo, I swear it.' Clasping his head in her hands, willing him to believe her, she told him again, 'I love you, only you, always you.'

His black eyes blazed at her words, and his huge body shuddered as he drove into her, filling her, utterly possessing her. 'At last, at last,' he groaned, in a voice thick with passion. 'I've waited so long...'

Then there were no more words, only two bodies entwined silk on satin, sweat-slicked, moving in the age-old primitive rhythm of ecstasy, until they reached the ultimate high: climaxing in perfect unison, spilling out their love for each other in a shuddering molten flood of passion.

'*Dio!* How I love you!' Carlo sighed deeply, fighting for breath as he collapsed against Helen. But she hardly registered his words, as, sated and barely conscious, she drifted into sleep.

Helen awoke the next morning to the intoxicating realisation that she had lain cradled in Carlo's arms all night. She sat up, careful not to wake him, his arms secure across her stomach. Slowly she allowed her eyes to wander over his sleeping form, exulting in the opportunity to study him unobserved. Some time during the night he must have put the coverlet over them, but it barely covered his thighs. His broad chest rose and fell steadily with his measured breathing. Somehow, in sleep, the harsh lines of his face appeared softer. His black lashes curved thickly over his cheeks like a child's. Helen ached to touch him, an invisible thread tugged at her heartstrings, and she was incapable of resisting the sheer magnetism of his virile form. Gently she bent her head and pressed her lips to the hollow between his shoulder and throat.

'Hmm, I should be awakened like that every morning.'

Helen jerked back, embarrassed to see Carlo wide awake, his eyes sparkling with amusement, and she blushed to the roots of her hair, as he laughed out loud.

'Oh, Helena, what am I going to do with you? Last night you were a complete wanton in my arms, and this morning you're blushing like a schoolgirl. Will the real Helena please stand up?' he mocked gently.

Fighting down the colour in her face, Helen responded cheekily, 'Well, if you let go of me, I would.'

Carlo's arm tightened around her, and his other hand reached out to push the tumbled mass of her long hair behind her ears.

'Ah, no, Helena, I will never let you go now. Not after last night. I did warn you,' he reminded her, pulling her down to plant a firm kiss on her mouth. She trembled at his touch, moving restlessly against him as she vaguely remembered something else.

'No denial. You are mine unconditionally?' he questioned huskily, with the barest trace of doubt discernible.

'Yes, yes,' she stated, the memory of their lovemaking unforgettable, and that was it. He had said he loved her, but in the dazed state she had been in, she was not sure.

'Last night, Carlo, when we... Well, when you...' She ground to a halt, not sure how to ask him.

'Go on, *cara*, what is it you want to know?' Carlo encouraged, his hand softly cupping her breast, thumb gently teasing the pink tip. Her reaction was instant, and hastily she closed her hand over his, stilling his seeking fingers.

'If you keep doing that I won't be able to ask you anything,' she said breathlessly. Then, bluntly, she continued, 'Last night, Carlo... did you say you loved me?'

'Don't you remember?' he grinned, his hand escaping from her hold and sliding to her stomach.

'I think I do, but at the time I wasn't in the state of mind to register what you were saying,' she admitted.

'How could you doubt I love you, Helena?' Carlo replied, lifting his hands, a palm either side of her head, forcing her to face him. 'I have loved you for years, *cara*; surely you knew that.'

'No, I thought you hated me, or at best were using me,' she murmured, mesmerised by the expression in his eyes.

'My God! You must be the only one who didn't know. I thought I was being blatantly obvious.' And, drawing her head down, he rubbed his lips softly on hers, mouthing gently, 'I love you, Helena, with every breath I take,' and for long moments there was silence, till Helen sighed, breaking the kiss and pushing away from him.

It was so easy to forget all that had happened in the wonder of her love for him, but there was too much she did not understand. They had to talk, get rid of all the ghosts before they could be completely happy. 'In Rome, Carlo, why...?'

He interrupted her, 'That week in Rome was the happiest time of my life,' he husked, increasing the pressure on her head with one hand easing her back down, his intention obvious.

'Yes, but Carlo——'

'OK, you're right, we need to talk, but I could think of better things.' He grinned wryly, pulling her down to his side so she lay in the circle of his arm, her head on his shoulder. 'When we first met, I couldn't believe my luck. You were my fantasy, everything I had ever wanted in a woman but never expected to find. When you agreed to marry me it was a dream come true. Fool that I was, I actually thought your being related to Maria was a bonus. It was only when I met your father that I realised how wrong I was. I couldn't believe it when he started raging about my wealth, morals, or lack of them, and vengeance. I wanted to laugh, until I saw your face and realised you were beginning to believe him. It was then that my dreams turned into a nightmare.' His arm tightened around Helen. She could feel the tension in him, and her own hand stroked across his broad chest in a gesture of comfort. She could feel his pain as her own.

'Oh, Carlo, I loved you from the first day I met you, and everything was so perfect. But when my father arrived that last day and was so angry, saying all those horrible things about you, I was so shocked, I—I didn't know what to think,' she stammered in her haste to explain, 'and you didn't bother to deny anything,' she sighed, turning her head to look up into his dark eyes.

'I didn't say anything,' he responded slowly, 'because I was struck dumb. It had never entered my head that your father would object. Call me arrogant if you like, but the past was over and done with as far as I was concerned, and in my conceit I thought your father would feel the same, and welcome me as a son-in-law. But I knew I was in real trouble when he mentioned the termination of his work permit. The look in your eyes chilled me to the bone. When you ran away, I wanted to follow you, but thought it would be better to try and convince your father first. I tried everything I knew to get him to believe I was genuine in my love for you, Helena. Maria returned and I thought she might help me, but true to form, she took one look at your father's face and ran into the house with the baby. God, Helena!' he groaned, tightening his arms around her, 'I did everything but get on my knees, and beg, to that man, and then I realised it was useless, the enmity between our families was too great, as was his possessiveness about you.'

Helen stirred restlessly against his warm body. 'You were right, but there were reasons for his possessiveness,' she said softly and, snuggling into the curve of Carlo's shoulder, she told him of her grandmother's revelations, and the conclusions she had come to herself, when she had examined her father's behaviour in the light of her gran's perception of him. Carlo's response was not what she expected, and she sat up in bed quite hurt when he laughed out loud.

'The old devil! God, I wish I had known that at the time. He wouldn't have refused me, then. What would his superiors have made of that?'

'Carlo!' she exclaimed. 'That's blackmail, you wouldn't!' but, staring down at him lying flat on his back, hands behind his head, she could see by the narrowing of his eyes that he meant it. 'You're really quite ruthless, husband mine,' she teased, not liking the bitterness she could sense in him.

'When it's something I want, I am ruthless, but that night useless would have been a better word,' he snorted disgustedly. 'Even you didn't believe me, the woman who was supposed to love me,' he stated, shooting her an angry glance.

The past still hurt, Helen thought sadly as, kneeling up in the bed, not touching him, she tried to marshall her thoughts. 'I should have trusted you, I know that now. But all I could think of at the time was that you had never told me, and how stupid I had been not to recognise that you were a wealthy man. I can see now that it wasn't important, and it was there for me to see, but I was blind. I felt so ashamed of my own behaviour. I think that was the worst part. Seeing my father made me a schoolgirl again, and I couldn't break in an instant a lifetime of his word being law. I suddenly realised how little I knew you, and how wantonly I had behaved. I was flooded with guilt; all the dire warnings of the nuns about the sins of the flesh rushed back to haunt me... I was too young, Carlo, everything happened so quickly.' She stopped, willing him to understand. 'I'm sorry you were hurt,' she whispered, as the thought of his accident came back to her.

'I wasn't hurt so much as furiously angry. My pride took a heavy battering that night. I had never pleaded for anything in my life before, and I didn't like the feeling. I left your villa in a towering rage, and when I woke up in the hospital I was still furious. A few cracked ribs and a cut didn't hurt half as much as losing you did. I bitterly resented the way you could turn me into a lovesick fool, and that was how I felt within twenty-four hours of leaving you.' The look he gave her was full of self-mockery, and, reaching up, he tugged gently on her hair, adding, 'And still do, woman. Come down here,' he drawled throatily.

But Helen was not prepared to let it go at that. 'Carlo, I know about your eye. Stephano told me.' Moisture hazed her lovely green eyes as she stared down at him. 'You loved flying, and now you are not allowed to and it's all my fault.'

'Stephano talks far too much. It was nothing—and don't cry,' he murmured gently, lifting his hand, and with one long finger removing a stray tear from her cheek. 'I really don't mind. I much prefer the way you make me feel to flying anyhow,' he declared soothingly, pulling her back down beside him.

For long moments they lay quietly in each other's arms. Heart to heart, hands softly caressing, not with passion, but with the easy familiarity of lovers, content in the knowledge of their openly declared love for each other.

'Carlo, why did you wait two years? If you truly loved me, why didn't you come to England?' Helen finally asked the question that had been nagging at her for weeks. With a groan Carlo turned her on her back, and leaning over her, supporting himself with an elbow either side of her head, he grinned wickedly down at her.

'You're determined to talk, I see, when I can think of much better things to do,' he opined, shaking his head in mock regret.

'Please, Carlo, I don't want any more misunderstandings.' Though his naked thighs rubbing against her own made her wonder if she could restrain herself long enough to listen! Carlo sighed, accepting that there was much to be cleared up between them, and slid down beside her.

'Well, at first, as I said, I was furious, but by the time Stephano came to the hospital on the Monday, I was desperate to see you. He went to the villa and of course found you had all left. That hurt . . .' he vouched, almost talking to himself.

Helen flinched at his words; the thought of him in hospital horrified her.

'By the end of the week I was back in Sicily, supposedly to convalesce, and though my body healed
quickly, my mind didn't. As soon as I saw Roberto I got
your address in England from him.' Helen watched him
study her; his piercing gaze reached right to her soul.

'Why didn't you answer my letter, Helena?' he
demanded.

She was stunned by his question and by the bitterness
evident in his tone. 'What letter?' she asked in
amazement.

'Don't lie to me, Helena, there is such a thing as
recorded mail,' he derided, his previous cynicism returning. 'I checked it was delivered to your home.' A
strong hand caught her shoulder, his fingers digging into
her soft flesh.

'Carlo, please, you're hurting me!'

If he heard her he gave no sign, but continued as
though she'd never spoken. 'God, Helena, you have no
idea what you did to me! I poured heart and soul into
that letter. Then I waited, the days turning into weeks,
the weeks to months, and every one longer than the last.
I couldn't believe you could be so heartless. I thought
the very worst that could happen would be a brief note
of rejection, but to hear nothing at all was even more
cruel ... I couldn't work, I couldn't sleep, each morning
I told myself, today I will hear from her, but it never
happened until eventually the hope turned to bitterness.
I thought of coming to England, of swallowing my pride
yet again, but by that time my father had had a stroke
and I could not leave him. For God's sake, Helena, why
didn't you answer me?' he demanded. His deep brown
eyes clouded with a lingering pain, and as Helen gazed
helplessly at him, she didn't know what to say.

'I—I didn't get any letter, Carlo. I swear I didn't.'
Stroking his still jaw with a slender hand, willing him
to be convinced, she added, 'If I had, I would have replied, truly, Carlo. I don't know what happened to it.
You must believe me,' she pleaded. 'I went to university

two weeks after returning home. I told you I travelled every day. I left the house at seven in the morning and never saw the mail. Perhaps it got lost at home somewhere,' she ended, her voice faltering as it dawned on her that probably it was something else her father had kept from her.

Carlo looked deep into her huge green eyes, and what he saw there told him she was telling the truth, and more.

'Your father again, Helena,' he stated.

'Probably. He said after Rome your name was never to be mentioned, and it wasn't,' she confessed, quietly.

'I should have guessed.' Carlo sighed and, holding her closer to his hard male form, kissed her with an angry passion, easing himself over her as he did so. Helen clung to him, her arms around his neck, returning his kiss with equal fervour, as though between them they could erase the bitter memories of the past two years. Finally Carlo lifted his head.

'I rang Maria, you know. Later in the New Year. She told me to give you time. She said she would try and bring you to Sicily in the summer, so I was prepared to wait. But after Roberto's death, when neither Maria or you turned up at his memorial service, I flew to England. I was going to talk to you, try and convince you how right we were together.'

Helen curled her fingers lovingly in his silky black hair. 'I wish you had, Carlo. I tried to do as my father said and put you out of my mind, but I think I always knew deep down inside that I loved you; I think I hoped you would come for me. What happened to stop you?'

'Nothing stopped me. I arrived the day of your father's funeral.' He favoured her with an ironic look. 'Hardly the time to demand you listen to me, hmm?'

She could see what he meant, she thought sadly. 'Still, I wish you had.'

'I might have done, even then, except I saw you walking into your house with a man.' His voice hardened as he went on, 'He had his arm around you, and I was consumed with jealousy, along with being furiously angry at being made a fool of again.'

'You had nothing to worry about! The man was Joe; he thinks of me as his daughter,' Helen explained.

Carlo smiled briefly, before continuing. 'Well, I came straight back here, determined to try and forget you, and with all the pressure of work and Roberto's death, it should have been easy, but it wasn't. Finally, at the beginning of this year, Stephano decided to take me in hand. He thought I needed entertaining, so he arranged a foursome. God, what a disaster that turned out to be.'

Helen stiffened at his words. 'Have there been many women?' she could not stop herself from asking, even though the thought hurt.

'Jealous, my darling?' Carlo asked, his eyes glittering with masculine triumph, then ruefully he added, 'You have no reason to be. I got the woman into bed, then nothing. I've never felt so embarrassed in my life. If I had seen you then, I would have killed you. For two years I've been celibate, so you have a lot of making up to do.' And, lowering his head, he gently brushed his mouth to hers.

'I'm sorry, Carlo, truly.' She was filled with awe that she could so affect this glorious male, and she couldn't stop the satisfied smile that spread over her face.

'Yes, you look it,' he mocked. 'After that episode, I think I did go crazy, and that was when I made my plan. I got the contractors started on this house, and set a detective agency on to finding out what you were doing. Then I bought Garston's and installed Stephano with strict instructions to employ you somehow,' he continued, adding happily, 'and it worked like a charm.'

'Oh, Carlo,' Helen exclaimed, laughing, 'and I thought it was all for revenge!'

'Oh, Helena,' he mocked, 'do you really think I would go to such lengths for a petty revenge? Don't pretend you don't know what you do to me,' and to prove his words, he rubbed sensuously against her, leaving her in no doubt of his claim. Then his mouth closed over hers, his tongue forcing an entry.

Instantly Helen was on fire for him, but determinedly she lifted her hands, pushing him away. There was something else she needed to know. 'On our wedding night, Carlo, why did you say you had waited six years?' It had hurt at the time and still worried her. 'Six years ago you didn't know me; you were engaged to Maria.

Carlo rolled off her, and supporting himself on one arm looked down at her in amazement. 'So that was why you went cold on me! God, Helen, how can you be so blind? Tell me, do you not recognise this bay?'

Of course, she thought, the stranger on the beach the last time she had been to Sicily with her father!

'It was you, the man on the beach,' she murmured.

'Yes, it was me. I saw you naked as a babe, running along the breakwater like a golden-haired sea-nymph. I was down here surveying the land with an option to buy, and I couldn't believe my eyes when you appeared. I thought I was dreaming. I watched you for ages, afraid to move, until finally I couldn't resist trying to speak to you, but as soon as you saw me you ran. I bought the land, of course, and for years you were my fantasy. I couldn't believe my luck when I met you in Rome with Maria,' he stated emphatically.

'You recognized me, after all that time?'

'Helena, I would know you if I was blind, deaf and dumb; you are my other half.' Deftly inserting a firmly muscled thigh between her legs, pinning her to the bed, he drawled throatily, 'Though I must admit I prefer to see you.' While his free hand lazily stroked her breast, one long finger pressing the sensitive nub, he studied her golden nakedness with reverent fascination.

Helen's body responded instantly to his touch, but there were still one or two things she wanted to know. 'Please, Carlo,' she caught his hand in her much smaller one, 'why were you so angry with me when we first married?' she asked rather breathlessly.

'Mmmm?' He lowered his head, murmuring, 'What was that?' as he covered her face and throat with tiny hot kisses, his hand sliding lovingly down over the curve of her hip.

'Carlo!' she squeaked, as his tongue licked over the hard peaks of her breasts. 'Please, I want to know.'

'God, woman, you're impossible,' he complained, raising his head to fix her with a baleful stare, but the light in his brown eyes told her he didn't mean it. 'That's why I was angry.'

'That what?' she asked, puzzled.

'Your stubbornness, woman, that's what. You must be the most stubborn woman in the universe,' he opined.

Her green eyes widened. 'I am not!' she declared indignantly. 'I just want to know...'

Carlo cut in. 'OK, I suppose I owe you an explanation. I was angry—bitter, even, but that was because you had effectively emasculated me—not, as you seemed to think, because I was out for revenge. The funny part is, I had only got engaged to Maria the week before I saw you for the first time. In fact, it was a relief to me when she ran off with your father. I'd known for ages I would never marry her.'

'Carlo, that's dreadful of you!'

'Stop interrupting, woman, or I won't say another word,' and with an exaggerated sigh he continued, 'All the time we were apart, deep down, I was sure you loved me. I told myself you were only eighteen and needed time, but I never doubted you would be mine in the end. That was why I agreed to your stupid bargain so readily. I reckoned once we were married and I got you in my bed, all my troubles would be over. Only it didn't work out like that.' Carlo laughed wryly, remembering. 'I could get you to respond, true, but always you held something back, and I wanted so much more, everything, in fact, and the more I took you the angrier I got as you refused to give in completely.'

Helen raised her hands to lightly stroke over his broad shoulders, knowing just what he meant, and Carlo grinned down at her in acknowledgement.

'I'm sure my shoulders must be marked for life, so determined were you to resist me, even though at times I was sure you were going to give in.'

She knew just what he meant; she almost had in the first few days, except seeing him with Caterina had stopped her.

'Anyway, by the night of Caterina's party I was desperate.' Helen stiffened in his arms at the mention of the other woman, just as she had thought about her. Her hands dropped to her sides, and Carlo felt her reaction.

'I've told you before, Helena, she is nothing to me, except the widow of my best friend.'

'But you told her about our marriage,' Helen couldn't help saying. 'That first Monday when I met you she said I was an obedient Sicilian wife—the exact same words you used.'

Carlo threw his head back and roared. 'So that was what upset you. Oh, Helena, I never mentioned you to Caterina, but that expression is a sort of standing joke among my friends. You know my father—well, for years he has been telling me to find an obedient Sicilian wife, and everyone knows that. It was pure coincidence that Caterina used those words.'

But she still wasn't satisfied. 'You told me that was what you wanted, when I first arrived.'

'Helena, I said and did a lot of things, some I'm not very proud of, but I was so determined to have you I didn't know what I was saying half the time. You have that effect on me,' he husked lightly, rubbing noses, before continuing. 'I know our wedding night was a disaster, and the next morning I lost my temper completely. I didn't hurt you?' he asked, rather belatedly, she couldn't help thinking.

'No, not physically, but my pride was shattered. I resented the way you could make my body respond to you.'

'I can, can't I, *cara*?' he drawled, grinning like a Cheshire Cat, his hand straying to caress her inner thigh, and it occurred to Helen that having this conversation in bed was not the best idea in the world.

'Carlo...' she admonished, grasping his wandering hand.

'All right, Helena. Seriously, that Saturday morning was inevitable, I think. It acted as a catharsis, purging me of all the rage and bitterness I had stored inside me for so long. I picked the red rose and vowed I would win your love again, and I thought I was succeeding. I had it all planned. On the Monday when I left you so obviously interested, I was on cloud nine. I intended to shower you in presents, a romantic dinner for two, then I would confess how much I loved you.' The look in his dark eyes as he spoke told her it was the truth. She raised one slender hand, gently tracing the outline of his brow. 'Carlo, you have your brown-velvet look back,' she whispered softly.

'Oh, Helena, it has always been there for you. Only you were too blind to see,' he said huskily.

'I'm sorry for doubting you,' she murmured.

'So you should be, woman. I could have strangled you that night,' he stated, some of his old arrogance returning. 'To a Sicilian male, respect is everything. I don't think I have ever been so insulted in my life as when you walked out of that shop,' he said grimly. 'How the hell could a few carelessly spoken words cause such trouble?' he groaned, adding, 'But then, listening to other people has been the root cause of all our problems,' and with a flash of bitterness he swore, 'What a waste, what a bloody waste of two years!'

Helen heartily agreed, and clung to him with a passion that matched his own as he forced her down into the mattress with the burning heat of his body and the fierce demand of his kiss. When he finally allowed her to catch her breath, Helen couldn't resist one more question, though she knew the answer. 'Would you really have taken Andrea?' she whispered, as he was about to kiss her again. She felt his withdrawal, even though his body never moved, and was immediately ashamed for asking him.

'How could you believe I would ever harm anyone so young and so close to you, Helena? Do you still not understand me any better than that?' he asked sadly, but before she could speak, he went on, 'I was desperate, and I used the only thing I could think of to get you to stay, but I swear I would never have gone through with it. You must believe me.' Carlo's dark eyes burned into hers, willing her to accept the truth of his words. 'I'm not proud of what I did, *cara*, in fact I'm ashamed of the way I treated you. Can you ever forgive me? Really forgive me?' he asked a slight tremor in his voice that he could not disguise.

Helen's heart swelled in her breast, flooded with love for this man, her proud, arrogant husband, who even after the night they had just spent was still not sure of her love.

'Oh yes, yes, Carlo. I never really believed you would hurt Andrea.' And as she said it she realised it was true. 'I think subconsciously I was glad of the excuse to stay with you. I love you, I always have, and always will, although I got sidetracked for a while,' she confessed huskily, emotion choking her. If she thought her words would finally convince him, she was wrong, she realised as he studied her intently, some slight reserve evident in his expression.

'If that is the truth, Helena, then why? Why yesterday, when I returned home, was I met with such icy indifference? You can't begin to know how that hurt. The only thing that kept me sane sorting out the mess half a world away from you was the thought of coming home with all our differences resolved. I almost gave up yesterday, when you told me you wanted to stick to that ridiculous agreement.' Gently stroking the soft plane of her stomach almost reverently, he asked, 'Was it the thought of having my child that frightened you so much?'

The worried frown marring his handsome face and the underlying concern in his voice filled Helen with shame. How could she have let him think that? 'No, Carlo. No, I want your child—our child,' she corrected quickly. 'I used that as an excuse, I'm ashamed to admit; it was Caterina,' she mumbled, turning her head to the side, unable to withstand his scrutiny. But he wasn't about to let her get away so easily, as he caught her chin and turned her back to face him.

'What in hell has the woman done now?' he demanded angrily, and Helen had no choice but to confess her stupidity.

'I rang your apartment on Friday night and she answered the phone. I know I was wrong, Anna told me last night that Caterina and Diego had married, but at the time I thought...' Her voice trailed off, leaving him in no doubt as to exactly what she had presumed.

'I've told you, she is nothing to me. I lent them my apartment in Rome before I knew I would be returning home that night. The other occasions I saw her were simply to try to persuade her to sell me Roberto's shares of the marina. Is that clear, *mia sposa*?' he mocked lightly.

'Oh, Carlo, I'm sorry for doubting you, truly I am, and I promise I never will again,' she vowed, the love shining in her wide green eyes, telling him everything he needed to know.

'Good. You should be, but I'm glad,' he declared, his dark eyes gleaming with wicked satisfaction. 'I like to think of you being jealous. God knows, I suffered enough!' and, rolling over on to his back, he pulled Helen on top of him.

'Now can we get on with the serious business of making love?' he asked sensuously, his mouth nuzzling her throat.

'But why did you want the marina?'

'I don't believe this, can't it wait? I have two years' enforced celibacy to make up for, woman,' he groaned in frustration.

Lying on top of him, Helen was perfectly aware of his condition, and teasingly moved her hips against his hard thighs, lowering her head, and whispering against his lips, 'I promise, not another question.' And as his arms closed around her, and he would have prolonged the kiss, she added, 'After you've answered.'

'You promise, this is the final, ultimate—no more?'

'I promise,' Helen vowed solemnly.

'Good. Remember when I said I wasn't expecting you here until November? Well, that was because I have been busy divesting myself of a lot of business interests. I intend to work only from Palermo, so I can spend more time with you. I have retained some speculative oil contracts; I can compete as easily from here as anywhere, along with the shipping line, as Palermo is the home port for the tankers, and the marina ties in very well. Your father was right, I do berth my yacht there most of the time, but I also enjoy building them. Now are you satisfied?' he demanded, twisting his hand in her hair, holding her face only inches from his.

'That's marvellous, Carlo! I hated the thought of your being away for weeks at a time without me,' Helen freely admitted.

Carlo, his dark eyes dancing, yelled, '*Finalmente*!' and tossed her on to her back, his full weight pinning her down. 'At last,' he groaned, like a starving man finally offered food, as his mouth found hers.

Willingly she gave herself up to the magic of his kiss. At last they were thoroughly secure in the wonder of their love for each other. Her hands clasped his wide shoulders, caressing down his broadly muscled back in an ecstasy of sensations. Fiercely they clung to each other, kissing, caressing, murmuring sweet words of love, in an orgy of giving.

Their hearts pounded as one, and Helen thought she had never heard such a wonderful sound.

Then suddenly she stiffened, her hands pushing at Carlo's chest instead of caressing.

'Carlo, someone's banging,' she said softly, her eyes darting to the still open bedroom window.

He raised his head, an expression of sheer disgust on his flushed face, and he groaned in pure masculine frustration.

Helen burst out laughing. 'Shhh... Listen,' she spluttered. Carlo turned his head towards the open window, and sure enough, there was a steady knocking.

'Oh, my God! I don't believe it, caught again,' he exclaimed and throwing back his head, roared with laughter.

'What is it?'

'I forgot—on the way home yesterday, I stopped off at an old friend's house, and arranged for him to come this morning, and engrave the plaque outside with your name.'

So that was why he was late yesterday, Helen thought, and, grinning up at him, she said cheekily, 'And that's my next question answered.'

Together they flung their arms around each other, rolling on the bed, convulsed in gales of laughter.

A bittersweet smile spread over the wrinkled face of the old man on the terrace as the sound of laughter floated on the still morning air. What wouldn't he give to be twenty years younger, or even ten? he thought, as he slowly chiselled into the stone, 'The Villa Helena'.

Can you keep a secret?

You can keep this one plus 4 free novels